Cathy,
there's no
room for error!

xMarino

Error

Adrenaline Series Book 5

Xavier Neal

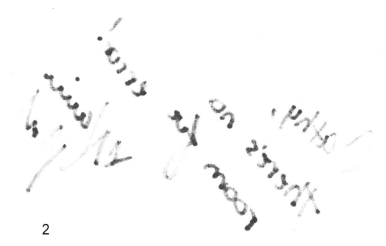

Error

Adrenaline Series Book 5

By Xavier Neal

© Xavier Neal 2015

Published by Entertwine Publishing

Cover by Entertwine Publishing

All Right Reserved

Dedicated to: The Universe. Thank you for letting me know there are no true errors, just learning chances.

Destin

There is a lot of internet porn out there. I mean a ridiculous amount. And I've clicked on some crazy sites. Have you ever seen a dude shove a fist up a chick's ass and spit on their own elbow? Oh you're not into that? Me either. Found that out the hard way during a battle with a bottle of whiskey. Lost twice that day. Hey, don't fucking judge. Have a shot with me instead. You know you want to. No? Fine. More for me.

Disappointed with my latest search results, I mindlessly reach for something to drink from my nightstand. The sound of crashing bottles causes me to flinch.

Fuck that was loud.

I glance at the mess and give my forehead a good rub.

This is clearly a sign I need to go out to have a drink, don't you think? Wanna join me? Wanna see me naked? Total possibility if you get me a little more drunk. What do you mean how drunk am I right now? Does that matter? You're not prudish are you? I don't wanna ride the prude train right now.

Clicking over from the open internet window of porn to the monitor I have set up. I watch the flashing dot of the tracking chip

6

we planted in a sculpture The Devil is now hauling around the country.

The Devil is a fucking nightmare. He gives an entire different vibe to the whole Devil Wears Prada thing. And yeah I know about that movie, my cousin Ben, who died a couple months ago, sat through it once to help him screw some chick. He was a freshman in high school and the girl he wanted to deflower required a little more effort than most girls who sleep with McCoys. Our reputation is enough. My point was...wait what was my point again?

I tab over once more studying the latest bank account of his I'm helping drain.

The Devil looks like a stock broker but behaves like a dictator at the end of his rope. To be fair, he's definitely creeping to that point. Over the past month, since his men killed one of my Triplet brothers, Daniel, I've passed the time drinking profusely and hacking into every possible thing I can involving him. Hacking is like breathing. It requires very little effort, but ripping rug after rug from underneath him has turned destroying his life into an Olympic sport for me. I want that fucking gold medal. This week alone I've forced three of his Swiss bank accounts to close, had two of his accounts here in the states frozen, and leaked to the Police Commissioner through an anonymous tip every location he has traveled to with the statue. Some of them are homes he hides in. Some have been allies.

7

Others just safety sanctuaries he thought he had discovered. Regardless, the rope around that smug fucker's neck is tightening. And I love it. Do they make platinum medals? They really should.

Without my eyes leaving the screen I lean down to search for another bottle of liquor.

I know I have at least a shot left in one.

When my efforts come up empty yet again, I grunt, shut my laptop closed and stumble off my bed.

Definitely think tonight is a good night to go out to the bar. Find a little something to bring home and bury my misery in. Daniel style....It's not like porn can touch me back and honestly? I think I'm getting callouses. Yeah. Exactly.

Azura

I have seen some crazy board designs, but why on earth would anyone want one painted to look like a bloody toe? That's just so gross. I don't know what's wrong with people. Is it supposed to be funny because you can break your toe skateboarding? Do they think that's ironic? It's not ironic. It's moronic. I can see how easy it is to get the two confused.

Scrolling down, I continue to review some of the designs I've seen on my client's boards. Frustrated, I lean back in my seat.

Is it so wrong to want something different? I blend in with everything else in life, it would be nice to stick out a little here.

"Hey," my step sister, Angela pops in my room, hand still gripping the door knob, eyes everywhere around my room, but on me. "Have you seen my lacy white top?"

I look away from the computer. "The see through one or the one that ties in the back?"

"Ties," she says in an indecisive voice, almost as if she doesn't believe it herself. "At least I think I'm looking for the one that ties. I'm pretty sure I let Lacey borrow the other one."

Angela is the definition of a goddess. Everything every guy typically dreams of. She's petite and not afraid of a push up bra. Blonde, mostly natural, but doesn't mind spending the extra few hundred bucks to truly bring out the color. Most importantly, and the biggest fact might I add, is she has no problem being proud of the fact she's easy. Yeah. She's proud *of that. She used to be Daniel McCoys "Tuesday Girl' when he was alive. Can you guess what she did on Tuesday afternoons? Sometimes I think she misses that more than she lets on. It's not like she talks to me about anything. Or even typically acknowledges I fucking exist. If she did, I would ask why she let herself be used like that. She's not a useless airhead with no future. She's actually really smart. We're talking a semester away from finishing her degree at med school, so she can finally ditch this city for one up north to complete her residency to become an obstetrician. That's right. She wants to help women having babies, but can't keep her own legs closed. Again, not quite irony, but at least it made you tilt your head a little in contemplation.*

Watching her search my room that looks military precision clean in comparison to hers, I shake my head. "No."

"Shit," she grunts. "How can I not know where it is?" Her search continues, this time invading my bed. "Tommy really likes me in that. Well...he really likes me in that before he likes it on the floor."

I scrunch my face. "That's...a lot of information."

As if completely unaware she is indeed in my room, she prepares to walk out of it, making sure to say, "We'll probably swing by the bar for a couple free drinks."

Upon her disappearance, I push my glasses up my caramel colored face and mutter, "Of course you will."

That's right ladies and gents. She's about to leave the house to finish her residency while I help kick drunks out of a fairly busy local bar. I love working at Mickey's. It's an odd home away from home. It helps keep my actual passion afloat and to be fair, it's gonna help get me an apartment so I can stop living at home. Oh, before you look at me like that, Angela and I both live at home for two reasons. The first, to save money. The second, our parents are rarely home. They travel so much this house is more like their vacation home rather than the one they live at. Since I can remember it's been that way. When we were younger, we had rotating nannies who kept an eye out on us. Sometimes I think my mother couldn't stand the idea of being around me too long. Even when she was home she kept her distance, unlike her husband who couldn't get enough of his little girl. Angela's dad, married my mom when we were both four. He does Pharmaceutical Rep. stuff, which I think is where her need to be in the medical field comes from. My mom on the other hand, she does website maintenance and updates for various small businesses. Hm. Funny how she managed to pass that love over to me. Though, I prefer to cut and edit videos. Documentaries. That sort of thing. Believe it or not, it's a little harder to find a use for my degree when every asshole with a camera or a cell phone puts up their shit on YouTube. And yes...I am on YouTube. Let's not talk about that.

A text causes my phone to vibrate across my desk.

Spencer: You're late for work.

Annoyed at the insistence of one of the only friends I have, that he knows me as well as he does, I type back.

Me: No.

After a quick glance at the time, I shout, "Yes! Shit!"

He types back immediately.

Spencer: You are terrible with time.

Me: Yeah. Yeah. I'll see you shortly.

I close the windows once more putting the things I love in life on hold for the things I do in life to get by.

Don't we all do that? Isn't that the definition of life?

**

"No. No. No." Ted, a retired Marine, and bar regular says to his buddy. "A chick like Azura is off the market. She just doesn't wear her ring."

Okay, so you see him right? He looks like he could be twins with Dwayne Johnson. He could eat me as a pre-workout snack and still be hungry. What? Oh the problem? He's not at all my type. Plus, it's best not to date the customers. I will be the first to admit he is one helluva good piece of eye candy though.

"Are you?" His friend flirts fixing his tie, making one very bad mistake.

Popping a hand on my hip, I shake my head. "No. But you are." When his eyebrows furrow, I tilt my head at his hand. "Faint tan line on your finger."

He quickly places it in his lap. "Good eye."

"Not my first day on the job." I wink. When Ted starts to laugh I ask, "Do you two need anything else right now?"

13

"Wings?" Ted suggests. His friends nod and Ted smiles at me. "You know how I like 'em."

With a friendly giggle, I prepare to walk away. "You bet your ass I do."

At the machine I put in his food order quickly and grab the bottle of Jack Daniels. Approaching Destin McCoy, who is at the opposite end of the bar from Ted, I dangle the drink in front of him. "Ready for a refill?"

"Nah," he hisses. "Didn't you hear? Jack and I broke up?"

I smile wide at his lame joke.

Ugh. Don't give me that scowl. I can't help it. Destin McCoy is not only one of the infamous McCoy brothers, he's a part of the even more legendary Triple D. Triplets so damn identical most people can't spot the differences. I guess when you've been longing for one in particular as long as I have you start to notice them. Sure his body has matching sleeve tattoos to his brothers and the thin yet muscular shape, but his eyes are more toffee colored than brown. He rocks a tongue ring when they're not busy trying to play live action three card monte with themselves. A tongue ring that if I do say so myself, I've spent many nights dreaming about between my legs. I

14

swear he owes me some serious cash back for the batteries I've had to buy. Mickey's is home to the McCoys as much as it is to me, and that's saying something. In general, I don't feel at home anywhere.

Attempting to flirt I say, "Sorry to hear that."

Destin shrugs and pushes his glass at me. "Shit happens. People leave you. Then you die. Whatever. Jim and I on the other hand, have started to fuck like crazy so if you could hook me up with that, it'd be appreciated. Ghost version if you've got it."

"Comin' up..." I sigh and turn to retrieve his request doing my best to ignore the comment that doesn't sit well with me.

I can't imagine the pain he's going through. God, I wish he'd talk to someone. Sad thing is it is the first time I've seen him since Daniel's death. How do you reach someone who barely registered you're alive before tragedy began to consume them? Who am I kidding? Aside from paying customers and video clients, no one registers I'm around.

Once the bottles have been swapped, I grab him a fresh glass and pour it on the rocks. Sliding it across to him, he wastes no time chugging it back. Without a word he taps the rim implying he wants it filled to the top.

Against my better judgment, I do. "Did you drive here tonight?"

He moves the glass away while looking over his shoulder. "Nope."

Disappointed at the known action, I sigh, "Well that's good at least."

Destin doesn't reply. He simply gives a wave to a blonde in a back booth who is there with what has to be a bachelorette party or sorority sister outing.

Good to know some things will never change.

Strolling away, I tend to the other bar members in between filling the incoming orders. The night continues on as smooth as any Friday night does. Business booms, drinks are demanded at outrageous paces, and I'm once again proud I've managed the art of handling the weekend alone.

It took some time but eventually Mickey trusted that I could manage being the only bartender on Friday nights. It does great things for my pockets, plus it lets me request many Saturday nights off without taking a hit.

Finally, it's last call and I'm thankful Ted typically waits until everyone is almost out before leaving himself.

We do have a bouncer, but Ted is convinced he scares no one.

Ted tilts his head towards Destin, whose head is lying on the bar. "You sure you got that?"

Giving a quick glance, I bite my bottom lip. "Yeah...I'll take care of him."

"I hear those McCoys are dangerous," he sighs. "Azura-"

"I've handled them drunk and sober." A small sigh comes from me as I look at him again. "Trust me. He'll barely even realize I'm helping him."

Ted hums, "His loss..."

When I turn back around I simply press my lips together.

Guess it's that obvious to everyone who is not *him.*

Slowly Ted exits the bar and into the fall night. After locking the door behind him, I finish the remaining closing duties while Destin simply drunkenly sings along to the radio that's still playing.

By the time I'm finished, I lie my head to face his from the opposite side of the bar. "Hi..."

"Hi...."

"You need a ride?"

"My lexabition to foqrukulate has failed."

Care to translate?

"I see. So, yes?"

"Yes," Destin whispers closing his eyes. "Or I can sleep here. Sleep here good."

My fingers twitch with the urge to touch his sad face. Instead I grip my keys tighter. "You know what's better than sleeping here? Sleeping in your bed."

"Bed," he repeats. "Bed. Bed good too."

"Is that a deal?"

Rocking, he manages to lift his head to agree, "Yes. You may take me to bed."

If only that was the invitation he was offering. Oh and of course I would prefer that invite to be while sober.

With a smile I hop on the bar, slide across, and slip his arm over my shoulder.

"Holy shit," he drunkenly mutters. "It's like you're an acromat!"

Before you ask me why I let him get this drunk, I didn't. I told his waitress to stop serving him liquor, which she did, but women kept sneaking it to him when they thought I wasn't watching. It's not like I could kick him out. I told you. Mickey's is home to the McCoys. Besides most nights he slips home with one of the groupies before that's even an issue.

I hum and help him through the back where Steve is waiting. Immediately puzzled at the sight he says, "You're not supposed to take them home, Azura. You're not a taxi service."

"Your head is shaped like a fushroom," Destin drunkenly declares.

Steve snaps as we approach my black car, "What the fuck is a fushroom?"

"A fucking mushroom?" I guess.

"No." He quickly shakes his head. "Whoa...mobo sickness."

Motion sickness. See. He's wasted.

"A fushroom, is the tip of your dick dude," the explanation clear as day. "Duh."

"Did he...did he just-"

"Yes," I cut him off. Opening my passenger side to help him in I politely say, "He did just call you a dickhead. However, he is way too gone to care. I'll make sure he apologizes the next time he comes in."

"Do that."

"Promise. Thanks again, Steve."

"Yeah," he grumbles backing up towards his motorcycle mumbling profanities under his breath.

His head does look a little funny shaped. But shhhh....

In the car, I help him get buckled in before allowing him to give me directions to wherever it is he lives. Destin spouts off a combination of clearly precise instructions and jumbled information that has me driving around in circles damn near delivering him to the wrong house multiple times. Once I'm finally flustered, I shoot Angela a text for an address. During the drive he fades in and out of sleep, at certain points I'm not sure if he's hitting on me or repeating lines from porn.

When I finally arrive in front of the McCoy Mechanic Shop, I manage to convince him to give me his keys. Of course the process is a difficult one filled with pouts and proclamations that I need to dig them out, but he eventually gets frustrated enough to just hand them to me. Once the door is unlocked we make our way toward the door at the top. The stumbling up a flight of stairs with a limp, swaying drunk takes more athletic energy than I've used in years.

It's not like I'm that out of shape. I skateboard sometimes. Keeps me kinda fit. Whatever. You help a drunk 180 pound weeble wobble up the stairs and we'll talk about my exercise regimen.

Unlocking the apartment that is above the shop, I'm startled by the crowd that appears to be waiting for us.

"Thank fuck," Madden, the oldest McCoy and by far the scariest, growls.

"Seriously," Drew, Destin's living triplet brother, sighs.

"Why didn't you answer your goddamn phone?" Madden bites harshly.

"Why the fuck aren't you home sooner?" Drew's concerned voice echoes.

Destin lifts his drunken face.

Knoxie who's not technically a McCoy, but might as well be, flops her face in her hand at the kitchen table. "No one is gonna thank the gorgeous nerdy girl who brought him home?"

"Thanks Azura," Drew whispers before folding his arms across his chest. "Appreciate it."

Destin wiggles himself away from me. "Don't fluckin thank her."

Drunk...he's drunk...remember that. Help remind me of that.

Drew lifts his eyebrows. "Excuse me?"

He turns to face me and flails around. "Tell 'em! Tell 'em your here to funk me-"

Instantly I surrender my hands in the air. "I swear, I was just driving him home."

Knoxie snips, "You sure you don't wanna sleep with Captain Morgan's taste tester here?"

"No Captain in me!" Destin snaps at her. "I sluck Jim harder."

"Oh...I'm so not touching that one," she mumbles and shakes her head. "Nope."

"And lore lying." Destin flails at me again. "You bo wanna fluck me."

I do, but not like this. Never like this.

"You bo wanna fluck me cause I look like my dead siplet who wouldn't fluck you if claid him."

23

As soon as the comment is out of his mouth my hand flies across his face.

Shit! That stings! A lot. Why didn't you warn me about the tingle? Oh I would do it again. You bet your ass. Oh my gosh, this hurts though...

"Shit!" Knoxie shrieks. "I felt that over here!"

Madden grouses, "That's enough, Destin."

"But-"

"Enough!" His voice bellows. "Take your ass to bed." Destin wobbles in objection, which is when Madden says, "Take your ass to bed before I lay your ass out to help you get there."

"Bye Bye Captain," he mumbles and starts to walk away.

Knoxie scrunches her face. "No one is gonna point out that he should've said Aye Aye Captain?"

"Knox," Madden snaps.

"Really? No one?"

Madden growls, "Knox…"

"Oh be a crabby patty all you want. You're not the only one still up at an hour that's strictly reserved for booty calls and IHOP employees, and still has to be up at an un-Godly hour for work."

The second she's finished, Drew insists, "Azura-"

"I know, Drew." Nodding slowly I put the keys down on the kitchen table and back up towards the door. "Still. I didn't deserve that."

Drew and Daniel both had a slightly more familiar relationship with me. They knew I brought them drinks. Daniel did try to sleep with me once, but he figured it out quite quickly he wasn't the McCoy for me. I saw him more often than the others thanks to his random pop in visits to Angela. He even told me once all I had to do was let him know when I wanted his help to hook up with his brother. I tried to explain I didn't just wanna sleep with him, but the concept didn't register. Yeah. That was Daniel. Female Angela in so many ways.

"No," Drew sighs. "You didn't…"

Turning the door knob, I prepare to leave. "I'm gonna go."

"I'll walk you down," he offers.

"I'm fine-"

"Let him walk you," Madden states.

He has this way he says shit. It forces you to comply whether it was your intent or not.

Drew motions at the door indicating he'll follow me. The two of us take the flight of stairs in silence. While the walk to my parked car is swift, it feels just the opposite.

Almost like the worst Walk of Shame you can imagine. None of the gain, all of the shame.

At my door, I politely say, "Thanks."

"Azura, listen," he starts slowly. "About what he said-"

"Drew-"

"Just let me finish," he implores. "He obviously didn't mean it, but I know that hurt. I know that hurt and I know *why* that hurt."

Pushing my glasses up my nose I try to act nonchalant. "I um...I don't know what you're talking about."

He smiles his award winning smiling. "If I wasn't in love myself I wouldn't fucking know it, but I am. So I do. All I'm saying is don't let some drunken outbursts put him out of the running. He's drowning. He needs a lifesaver. I think it's you."

With hope coursing through my blood almost as sharply as disgust, I somehow manage to nod.

I know he's right. Destin needs someone more than ever. All the death that keeps surrounding him, who wouldn't need a little help to not suffocate in that? What do you think I should do?

Destin

Who is fucking playing the bongos? Who the fuck even plays the bongos anymore? What do you mean those aren't the bongos? How could that possibly be my head? Why are you yelling? Seriously, take it down to below fog horn level.

Suddenly there's a sharp pain in my cheek and I shoot up. "What the fuck!" My own shouting makes me groan in further pain as my head hits the pillow again. Grumbles and mumbles fall from me while my body debates which pain sucks more.

Don't laugh, it's not funny. Huh? That's not you is it?

I open my eyes back up, despite their best efforts to stay closed, to see Knox staring at me with a smirk from the edge of my bed.

"Hi!" She shouts.

Still groaning, I reach for a spare pillow. Like she's got an NBA ring for blocking, she swats the pillow forcing it to fly out of my hands. When it hits my closet door, I cringe at the sound. "Damn it, Knox."

"Rise and shine Prince of The Distillery. Kitchen. Now." She rises off the edge of my bed, so I roll over, which is when she adds, "If you don't get the fuck out of that bed in the next forty five seconds, I will knee you in the nuts so hard it'll make your jaw click."

Is that possible? Ya know what? Never mind. I don't wanna fucking find out.

Somehow I manage to put on a pair of shorts that were on the ground beside my bed and wander into the kitchen where my family awaits.

Well, what's fucking left of it.

Reluctantly I slide into the seat at the kitchen table that's oddly enough not occupied.

Do you get the feeling they did this shit on purpose?

Madden who is leaned against the counter by the stove approaches, the vicious look on his face enough to make my stomach churn. When his large palms land on the table across from me, I fly backwards, the motion causing me to hold a fist to my mouth to stop the vomit.

"Oh God yes," Knox encourages from the area my big brother was just standing at. "Please puke in his face. I need something funny to get me through the day."

His eyes pierce mine harder.

It's like he's pushing the bile back down my throat. Scary fucker huh? Tell me about it. At least he's not breathing down your neck right now. Wanna swap? I really could use the rest.

"Let me make something crystal fucking clear to you," he starts slowly. "This stops now."

Perplexed, I shrug. "What does?"

"Your obsession with bringing down The Devil is beginning to get the better of you. Day and night, all you do is sit in that room-"

"Which smell horrendously by the way," Knox calls from over his shoulder.

"-and watch the screen while drinking yourself into a coma. No more. You wanna drink? Fucking fine. Do it with other people. You wanna hack? Fine. Do it for whatever reasons you used too. But hunting The Devil that way stops now."

30

Anger surges up my throat blindsiding the vomit. "Are you fucking kidding me? I've made so much goddamn progress! We're so fucking close to taking that asshole out!"

"We're not any fucking closer," Madden announces. "The only thing you're stalking has done is speed up the process of which the cops collect evidence on him and slowly, but surely start to kill my younger brother. You're done, Destin. I'm not about to lose another brother to him."

"So you're done? Just like that?" I snap. "He's killed my brothers, Madden!"

"Our." His finger taps the table. "They were my brother's too. And I'll let him kill me before he kills another." The cold words clamp my mouth shut. "We will figure out something else. *Together.* Not you, alone locked in your room like a serial killer in the making, but together, as a family. So let this go and get your life back together." At the end of his speech he backs up towards the front door. "You're not allowed in the shop today."

"But-"

"Drew's gonna cover for you."

31

"We need all hands. We're short," I remind him trying to hold back a sniffle.

"We'll deal." He assures with a cold stare. "Get your shit together, Triple D."

Madden exits without another word, slamming the door harshly behind him.

Knoxie sighs, "You know what the problem with you McCoys is?" When my face moves to look at her she shakes her head. "You're all so goddamn selfish. You're all in such a rush to dive on a fucking sword like you have to crucify yourselves for your lives to matter. You don't. They already do. You just fail to see it."

"Knox-"

"Don't." She lifts a hand. "I'm not in the mood." With one final shake of her head she mutters. "I have to get to work. Ya know, that place with the loud noises and annoying people."

As soon as she's out the door, Drew gets up from the bar table and relocates to sit across from me.

"You gonna chew me out too?" I grunt.

"Hey Mel," he says sweetly to his girlfriend that's lingering beside where he just was. "Can you give us a minute alone?"

"Sure," she softly replies. "I'll grab a shower."

He nods and watches her walk out of the room. The second it's just the two of us he asks, "Do you remember anything from last night?"

My brain struggles to put together pieces of anything after I crashed the birthday party of blondes.

Truth is, I'm the least smooth of all of us. I know, with a face like this it shouldn't be that hard. It's not. Between the well-known looks and even more well-known name, chicks kinda just drop in my lap. Daniel did the hard work, Drew picked what he wanted, and I just hung out with whatever was left. It didn't always end in sex, in fact more times than not it didn't....but I never had to go out and search for girls on my own. Beauty of being identical triplets. If they wanna fuck your brother, there's a good chance they wanna fuck you too. Flying solo is much harder. Some sort of whiskey last night helped me forget what rejection feels like.

"Yeah I didn't think so," Drew sighs. "You know Destin, I know what it's like right now. I get it. I lost him too." Uncomfortable by the words I shift in my seat. "There's this weird...void on the inside, you don't quite understand. This little piece of you that's just waiting to be filled again, but you know it never will be. You hear his laugh at dirty words or words that possibly sound that way. You see a blonde chick and first thing you do is the Daniel triple B check list because-"

"A Triple D should never settle for anything less than a triple B."

Beautiful. Blonde. B Cup. She can be more than a B Cup but never less.

Drew chuckles a little, "Exactly. Without him, it feels like there's a giant gaping black hole waiting to suck you in, so you compensate for his absence by doing things he would've. You try to recreate parts of him to keep him here. The porn. The drinking. The attempts at random one night stands."

Did you know I hate one night stands? I haven't had any recently either.

He leans in closer to me. "You're not the only one hurting, Destin. *I watched him die.*" The fact brings tears to both our eyes. "*I* watched him take his last breath. You are not the only one who is suffering with this, but you know what? I wake up every morning to the most beautiful woman in the world who reminds me that I'm not

34

alone. I still have another triplet brother. Truth is, if you keep this shit up I'm gonna end up without either of you. I miss Daniel as much as you do, but not enough to give you up in exchange. Stop trying to become him and be *you*. You're still here. You're still alive. Let's try to make the most of that...."

Drew extends his fist across the table for me to bump. I do.

This ladies, is the level headed triplet. Daniel was the wild one. Drew the reasonable one. I'm obviously the dashing one....Did you smile? Good. I did too.

"One more thing," Drew starts almost immediately smiling. "You were a douche last night."

Not surprised, I rub the side of my head. "To?"

"Azura."

My shoulders slump.

Look, Azura is not only the world's most gorgeous bartender in the history of human existence, she's also the kindest person I've ever met. I swear, if Daniel hadn't already slept with her...I...I am totally not finishing that sentence.

"Yeah. You um, said she only wanted to bone you cause you look like Daniel."

I grit my teeth. "I said that out loud?"

He nods. "Yeah."

"To her?"

"Yeah."

"Out loud to her?"

"No matter how many times you break down the sentence, the answer is yes."

Vomit jerks back up my throat.

"You need to call and apologize."

"I don't have her number."

Drew tilts his head at me. "You're gonna tell me that's an issue for you? How did you make sure you were in Mary Ann's English class again? It was really random luck of the draw your classes got scheduled that way?"

"Point proven."

"And you should know something else."

"What's that?"

"You're wrong."

"About?"

"Her." Still confused I wave a hand around. "It's not Daniel, she wanted to sleep with you. It's you bro."

Immediately I deny, "Nah..."

"Trust me." Drew smirks again. "I know a thing or two about chicks."

"Just 'cause you're practically married now doesn't mean you know shit about chicks."

He lightly laughs and stands. "To teach you just how much I indeed know about them, I'm gonna go fuck my girl rotten. Take notes."

"Ugh," I groan and let my head fall forward.

Before he leaves the room he gives me a strong pat on the shoulder and informs, "There's HS in the drawer."

Thank fuck. Hangover Serum is this little mixture Mel, his girlfriend, created that wipes the thing away. Man, it could make her billions if she sold it, but that's not possible...before you ask me why not, that's not my story to tell. It's hers. Now if you'll excuse me, I'm gonna grab a dose of that and figure out a way to undo the damage I'm sure I've done.

**

Bouncing on the balls of my feet, I try to battle away the trepidation that this is going to be as awful as I've imagined it in my mind.

And I've imagined quite a few different ways this scenario could play out, including having her ripping my nuts off and juggling with them. Thank God she's not Knox or that would be a real possibility.

I knock on my forehead twice and then the door.

To my surprise it swings open almost instantly. Angela gasps at me. "Daniel?"

"Destin."

My correction paints a familiar sadness into her eyes.

She was one of his regular girls. While he cycled through one nightstands enough to make anyone's dick scared of the outcome, he also had a handful of girls he called at routine times on certain days. They were his staple chicks. Judge him all you want, none of them fucking minded.

"Right." She shakes her head quickly. "I'm sorry. I just...you just...right. What's up?"

Nervously, I fidget. "Is your sister home?"

She hums to herself. "That's a good question." Contemplation rolls across her face. "Is her car in the driveway?"

I glance over my shoulder. "There's a black Honda Civic."

"Yeah, that's hers," she brushes it away with gag. "She must be in her room. Come on in."

Crossing the threshold, I immediately admire the extensive shot glass collection that covers the walls to the right. The entire area looks like it's intended for entertainment with the bar, the piano, and the chairs, but the floor to ceiling wall of glasses makes me wonder who in their right mind would trust drunk people in here.

I point. "The collection-"

"My dad's and he's rarely home." Angela bites her bottom lip and lifts her eyebrow. "Like now..."

Is she coming onto me?

Nodding, I let her lead me down the hall to where a large living room and huge kitchen intersect. We take a right. Along the walls my eyes can't help but fall onto the family photos. Many of them are just what I assume are their parents. The others mainly include Angela. Almost none of Azura.

At the end of the hall, before the path branches off to the right, she says, "You sure it's her you're looking for and not me?"

I clear my throat. "Positive."

"Well if you change your mind, just let me know." Unsure of how to take that I keep my mouth closed. "Anyway this is her. Just go in."

Curiously I question, "She won't mind?"

"I doubt it," Angela brushes off and starts walking towards her own room. "She rarely does."

I know they're only step siblings, but still. Do you get the feeling they're almost like weird college roommates?

On a deep breath, I twist the door knob to enter. To my pleasant surprise, I catch a glimpse of the most amazing set of tits I've ever seen. Period.

The enjoyment is beyond short lived by the shrieking and high pitched demands to leave. "Get out! Out! Out!"

Quickly I shut the door and lean my forehead against it. "Sorry..."

"What the hell are you doing here?" she yells from the other side. Before I have a chance to answer she jerks the door open. "And are you allergic to knocking?"

"Angela said-"

"Of course she did." Azura folds her arms across her chest. Anger seems to be disappearing just at the sight of me. Kindly she greets, "Hi..."

Loving the simple way that word sounded off her full lips, I repeat back, "Hi..."

A bit of tension builds, she asks, "Why...um..why are you here?"

My face tries to offer her a smile. "I came to apologize."

Suddenly her body relaxes and an odd wave of relief washes over me.

Fuck. I wasn't aware that I cared this fucking much about her being pissed at me. What do you mean of course I do? You barely know me. But yeah. I really did.

"I uh...I'm really sorry about how I acted last night. What I said..."

She whispers, "I know."

"I didn't mean it."

A small smile comes to the pair of beautiful lips I wanna stroke with my tongue. "I know."

"Wanna let me make it up to you?"

Azura slips her hands in the back pocket of her jean shorts. "How?"

"Lunch?"

My small offer gets a big grin. "Like a date?"

"Uh..." I shrug. "I uh...I guess?"

Why are you looking at me like that? Did I mess that up? Well I didn't expect I'd have to call it a date! I just- Well I- Would you stop yelling at me already?

Sweetly she sighs, "It's cool Destin. You don't have to pity ask me out-"

"That's not pity," I immediately spew. "I just..I haven't legit asked a girl out in a while, so I guess I just clammed up. But yeah. A date, Azura. That's what I want."

This time she wets her lips before grinning. "I want that too."

"Yeah?"

"Yeah..."

For a moment I just stare uncertain of what to say or do next.

Why am I so awkward? Why didn't Drew prep me better for this?

"But um...not today," she says. "I have plans."

Jealously instantly floods my system. "Like another date?"

Azura continues to smirk but shakes her head. "No. Just a party."

With a smirk of my own I playfully suggest, "I could be your date to that."

A doubtful look falls on her face seconds before she shakes her head profusely. "No. No. No. No....I don't think that's a good idea."

"Creepy ex-boyfriend gonna be there?"

"No."

"Stalker?"

"No."

"Secret twin sister you've been keeping from us with vampire teeth and hump back?"

Azura erupts into laughter trying to deny my suggestion in the process. Loving her laugh, I soak in every bit of it I can. For the first time in weeks, I can see my old self coming back on the horizon.

"Let me tag along," I encourage.

"It's a pool party. Do you have swim trunks?"

"I..."

Shit. I don't.

"I do have money though. We can swing by the store and I'll grab a pair."

Azura shakes her head. "Let me see if I can save you twelve bucks."

Intrigued I dart my eyebrows down.

"Angela!" she calls out. Nothing happens, so she repeats her name, "Angela!" The two of us wait in silence for a few moments before she yells it again, "Angela!" Finally her sister's door flies open and she asks, "You got a pair of swim trunks Destin can fit in?"

I look over my shoulder to see her in less clothing than she was before.

Sports bra and booty shorts. I pray she's about to work out and not try to seduce someone. They wouldn't stand a chance. Well, I would. No offense to my brother and his blondes are perfect policy, but I'm starting to think brunettes do it better. Particularly wavy haired ones.

She slides her hand up the door frame to pose, eyes planted on me. "Daniel's size, right?"

Nope. That's not happening. Not sleeping with her.

"Right."

She lingers for a moment before giving up. "Yeah, give me a sec."

As she disappears into her room, I turn around and analyze Azura's outfit. "You're not gonna wear that top are you?"

She looks down at the monstrosity, which looks more like a tank top than one that belongs in the water.

"What's wrong with it?"

"Not to sound rude, but you're working with an A plus rack in a C minus top."

Her caramel colored face flushes. Something inside of me whispers that I want to see her do that again and again.

Preferably while calling out my name and clawing at the sheets. Damn I'm hornier than I thought.

Angela comes down the hall dangling black swim trunks from her fingers. "These should work."

Politely I thank her, "Thanks."

"No problem." After letting her eyes dangle in mine a little too long, she gives her sister a look. Quickly she shakes her head. "No Az. We've talked about this a million times-"

"You mean you've said this a million times," Azura mumbles.

"That swimsuit top should be left at the bottom of the ocean so sharks can wipe their asses with it."

I point. "What she said."

"Ugh," Azura grunts before pinning me with an unhappy expression.

"You have a great set of boobs. Showcase them sometimes," Angela states as she walks off.

Smirking wider, I look at Azura cockily. "I definitely agree with that."

She rolls her eyes, but smiles brightly. "Fine. I'll change. You can use the bathroom right next door to do the same."

With one more nod, I follow her instructions, actually excited for the first time since Daniel died about something that doesn't involve hunting down one of the most wanted criminals in the country.

Who knows, maybe this excitement could lead to naked excitement. Can't blame a guy for hoping. I'm really trying to get away from watching so much porn.

Azura

One word. One word I never thought I would ever hear Destin McCoy say. Date. Well, say to me I guess I should correct. I've heard him say he has a date with many different drinks and the toilet several times in the couple years I've known him. Never a girl though. McCoys have never been big into dating. I remember when Merrick started. It was a phenomenon that gave me slight hope that someday, through a parting the sea kind of miracle, maybe the others would follow in his footsteps. Hope he's resting in peace.

After gently placing my bags in the backseat, one which contains my photo equipment and the other a dry pair of clothes for the event after, I move to the driver's door.

Unexpectedly Destin stops me. "Wait."

With my key in hand ready to go, I freeze.

"Maybe I shouldn't go."

Yup. Knew this shit was too good to be true.

Swallowing my fear I nod. "Okay."

His eyes that were just plastered on the ground clearly not here in the present with me shoot up to meet mine. "It's not that I don't wanna go with you."

The reassurance makes me bite my bottom lip to resist smiling. "But?"

He lets out a heavy sigh. "You wanna know one reason I like to stay locked up in my room behind the computer screen?" When I nod he says, "Because it doesn't offer me half ass condolences. It doesn't pretend to know how I feel. It doesn't offer me sympathy sex or sympathy shots or give me that judgmental look at the pathetic state of suffering my life is in. As much fun as a pool party sounds and the idea of hanging with you for the afternoon is....more than tempting, I just don't know that I'm ready to go through another dose of that stale bogus 'sorry for your loss' bullshit."

At that moment I take a long hard look at him knowing he's right, knowing I'm guilty of that very thing.

Of course I feel sorry for him. And of course I wanna try to comfort him that way, but from the looks of it, that's clearly not what he needs. He's craving normalcy. Maybe even a bit of invisibility. Now that's my specialty.

"One of the drawbacks of being a McCoy," he mumbles resting his arms against my car. "Everyone knows."

"Not everyone." My words wrinkle his forehead. "What if I take you somewhere that you're a little less than legendary? A place where you can say your name and people probably won't blink twice."

"Is that because they haven't found life on Mars yet?" When I giggle he adds, "And you said swim trunks, not an astronaut suit."

With another laugh I roll my eyes. "Just...shut up and trust me."

Destin wiggles his tongue around, the small ball of his piercing flashing itself at me in such a fashion, I have to force myself to look away. Sweat suddenly breaks out across my neck.

No. It's not that goddamn hot outside. You mean to tell me you don't wonder what that feels like in the very places I'm sure I'm collecting dust?

He gives me a grin. "Alright. I trust you."

"Good." I smile back. "Now get in the car."

The trip across town is actually more pleasant than I've dreamed of. We spend most of the time playfully arguing over the radio, his inability to sing though he swears he sounds just like the lead singer from Journey, and why AC is always better than the wind for cooling down.

"It's a bike thing," he says in a playful sneer, checking his phone for the fourth time.

"Well I wouldn't know. I've never been on one."

Immediately he tosses his hands in the air. "Exsqueeze me?"

"You want me to squeeze you?"

"Later if I'm lucky." Once I'm blushing he chuckles and adds, "You've seriously never been on a bike before? How is that possible?"

"I like things with four doors," I reply pulling up to the gated off neighborhood. "I feel safer."

"You'll feel plenty safe on the back of my bike. Trust me. Pepper and I will take good care of you."

Once I've entered the code, I turn to him. "Pepper?"

"My bike."

"Yeah, I got that. Why'd you name her Pepper?"

"Like Pots."

"From Iron Man?"

"You know comics?" His eyes lift as his face lights up. "Or from the movies? Tell me you know comic books."

"Guilty." I surrender a hand. "Avid lover. Even the less known ones like Commander Planet-"

"From the Onyx galaxy," Destin finishes for me on a chuckle. "I love Commander Planet!"

"Shut up," I whisper turning down the road that's only home to one house. "You're serious?"

"Yeah." He eagerly nods. "Remember that issue where he had to face the choice to save his own planet from the Death Ray of Red Mist or Louise Anna from Silver Storm?"

Too astir, I can barely contain myself as I park the car. "I do!"

"I liked that even when he had to face saving the world or saving the girl, he chose to save the girl."

Intrigued I face him. "Why?"

"Because to him she was his whole world. And one without her wasn't worth living in. Not fair to the billions of other people on their planet, but I try to imagine if he would've let her die, what would've kept him stepping up to keep up the fight after that? Sometimes just one person can push the entire course of history. Sometimes just saving one, saves them all."

Destin's eyes linger in mine, the toffee color that's close to my skin tone now returned. I admire the face I've spent years staring at, years waiting to notice me, finally doing just that. The magical feeling is overwhelming, intimidating, and intoxicating.

Oh boy. I'm in trouble.

"We should um...get going," I softly suggest.

The two of us head towards the Tudor style mansion where we bang a left instead of going through the front door. We follow the path around to the back where music is blaring and there's obviously a very lively crowd.

Steps before we enter, Destin asks, "How do you know these people?"

"I-"

"Took your sweet ass time getting here." My other best friend Jamie snaps rushing towards us.

Jamie, while I love her to death and she has been my best friend since I turned twenty one, is way too over protective. At 5'11 with a body builder figure from hours of MMA training and underground fighting, it's safe to assume it's not just her mouth that scares most people away.

"Any longer I would've sent out a search party to pry you away from your computer. I'm tellin' you, unless that thing learns to blow your back out, there's no reason to spend that much time on it. Work or not. "

Clearing my throat I correct her, "I was actually having a wardrobe crisis."

"Is that why you don't look like Mary Teresa today?"

If I had any chance at trading her for someone else, right now, I would.

Embarrassed I snip, "Jamie!"

"I like you," Destin laughs before extending his hand. "I'm Destin."

"I'm a lesbian," she informs shaking it back.

With a wide smile he states, "Lucky girls. However, I didn't mean it like I was hitting on you."

"He hated my top too," I quickly rush the words out. "A lot."

"A man with taste." Jamie lifts her pierced eyebrow. "Impressive. Do you like 'em tall, blonde, and members of the itty bitty titty committee?"

"Jamie!" I snap this time louder.

Destin laughs again this time sliding a hand around my lower back. Chills litter my skin. "Actually I prefer them like I do my scotch. Brown, smooth, and easy to go down."

57

Feeling my own face turn vinous, I bury it in the crook of my elbow.

Down on him? Or down on me? Does it matter? He wants someone to go down somewhere. Is it bad I'm all for that?

"Oh, I like you too," Jamie insists. "Besides any person who can make Azura turn that color without trying is someone to have around."

Destin nudges my hip with his body. Slowly I look up over my lowered glasses as he says to me, "I hope so. I like being around."

She motions her hand towards the entrance. "Then right this way."

All three of us stroll in the party together. The oasis most commonly referred to as a backyard is lively. To our right is the outside living space that stretches the length of the side of the house. It's separated from the inside by glass doors and windows. The overhead space has mood lighting while the area is decorated with everything from bar top tables which go along with the full bar service, to long lavish couches. Running parallel to it is a hot tub area which runs off into a luxury pool down beneath. In the distance is the golfing range, covered massage area, another bar, a sand volleyball pit and regular basketball court.

You're pretty much looking at what happens when you can't decide on one thing, so you pick everything.

Destin whispers in my ear, "Where the hell are we?"

"Preston Wyatt-"

"Wait." He grabs my arm. "Are we talking action star Preston Wyatt?" Before I can finish nodding he snaps, "No fucking way! No fucking way! How do you know Preston Wyatt?"

"Short version? We share similar tastes in recreational activities."

Outside of stunts on the screen, he likes extreme sports. Watching. Occasionally participating against his agent and lawyer's wishes.

Destin's tattooed arms fold firmly across his chest. "Are you trying to tell me you get high together?"

Mimicking his action I bite, "Really? Do I look like that kinda girl?"

"No but-"

"Destin," I cut him off. "I don't do drugs. I rarely drink. I only come to these types of parties because Jamie insists. Or Angela, like I did to Vinnie's party, even then she just wanted someone to drive her. With one exception, I'm a fairly boring person."

Oh geez....I shouldn't have said that. He doesn't want boring. No one wants boring. Why am I hell bent on self-sabotage?

"Why don't you let me be the judge of that?" Destin says, his arms falling as he approaches me slowly. "And um...what's the exception?"

"There's my girl," a loud voice over my shoulder coos. Quickly turning around, I see Spencer holding out a plastic cup. "I was wondering where you were. Your concept of time really does suck."

Before I can say anything, Destin snaps, "Your girl?"

Oh no...this... it's not what it looks like. I swear!

Spencer steps to my side. "Who the hell are you?"

60

"Who the fuck are you?" Destin steps closer.

Quickly I introduce, "Destin meet Spencer. Spencer meet Destin."

"Her date." He immediately extends his hand. "Pleasure."

With a disgusted look he hands me the drink. "Your date?"

"I'm allowed to date," I sigh, gripping the cup tighter. "Thanks for the drink."

"I thought you didn't drink," Destin interjects.

"It's a Shirley Temple," Spencer answers turning his attention to him. "You'd know it's her favorite if you knew anything about her besides her measurements."

He winks. "Which are exquisite by the way."

I cannot believe he saw me topless today.

Spencer grunts just as Jamie returns from wherever it is she wandered away too. "Oh look. A pissing contest. Who's winning?"

"Jamie," I whine.

Don't say she has a point! I know she has a point.

"It's all good," Destin assures. "There has to be a loser." Taking my hand he smiles at Spencer. "At least you did it gracefully. Now, are we heading down to that pool or what?"

Jamie chuckles and turns to lead the way. Spencer gives me the sympathetic puppy dog look I know all too well.

No we've never hooked up. No I've never thought about it. It doesn't mean he hasn't tried. Spencer was that nerdy kid in high school that got super gorgeous during his college years. We lost touch after we graduated and when he walked back into the bar a couple years ago, we caught up and started hanging out. In high school we were two dorks in a pond, but I never felt anything romantic. He assumed it was because of how he looked, however he was so wrong. There's no chemistry. Can't fake that. It's not an orgasm. Oh. Shit. No. I've....this conversation is over.

After shedding the clothes covering our swim suits and the guys measuring each other with harsh looks once they're shirtless, we dangle our feet in the edge of the pool.

"Killer rack at 12 o'clock," Jamie comments leaning back on her palms. "What I wouldn't give to motorboat those bitches."

Accustomed to her crazy word vomit, I simply snicker and shake my head.

"Is that all you think about?" Spencer gripes from the other side of her.

"Why is that *not* all *you* think about?" She quips in return. "Man, what I wouldn't give to know how many drinks it would take for her to 'get drunk and go a little wild'. I am not opposed to using that to my advantage."

Destin chuckles and replies, "Two mojitos and a two shots of tequila."

Jamie's eyebrows dart up. "For real?"

He gives her another look. "Yeah. You might wanna go one more shot for good measure, but that should do it. It's just the right amount of lowered inhibition for her to test the water."

"And how the hell would you know?" Spencer leans around Jamie to snap. "Fucked her before? I wouldn't be surprised. You seem like that type."

"Spencer!" I snap.

Destin slips an arm around my waist. "It's cool, Azura. To be fair, I know I look like that type."

Am I crazy? He is a McCoy. His brothers, no doubt have banged enough chicks to enter what is known in the dude world as Legendary Status, but for some reason I'm hoping he's different. Maybe a little different? At least a handful away from the status. Is there any possibility I'm not about to be another check box completed for Bang Girl Bingo?

"But no. I haven't slept with her."

"Then how do you know?" Spencer pushes. "Or are you talking out of your ass to get Jamie to like you?"

"Jamie doesn't like anyone," I mumble lifting my cup.

"Oooo that's true," she agrees. "People typically suck. One reason I enjoy hitting them in the face."

Baffled I shake my head. "Yet you like parties."

"There are chicks at parties. I like chicks. Simple. Logic."

Destin laughs again and pulls me in closer. The gesture so simple, so sweet I'm almost afraid of how incredible it feels. Almost too natural. Too perfect. "Truth is, I had a brother who fucked for sport. After fucking more than any man should be proud of, he had how much liquor was too much for what body/personality type down to a science. At one point he insisted on creating a pie chart to demonstrate. We managed to talk him out of it, so he used pizza instead."

Daniel McCoy gives a perfect face to sexually charged insane doesn't he?

"Point is...certain girls who are of certain sizes who carry themselves in certain ways can be given an educated guess of how much is too much," Destin continues. "There were always exceptions to the rule but for the most part, he wasn't wrong."

"That's bullshit," Spencer croaks out.

"That's genius," Jamie gushes.

I put my cup down and bury my face in the palm of my hand.

Why can't we have normal topics of conversations?

Destin laughs from beside me, the hand that was just stroking my side now running it's fingers across my exposed upper back. Suddenly he leans over and whispers, "I'm sorry for this."

Dropping my hand, I look at him kindly. "It's not your fault."

"Oh...it definitely is," he whispers as he smirks.

Unsure of what he means, I open my mouth to question him when he pushes me forward into the pool. Immediately darting to the surface, thankful my glasses stayed on, I shake the water out of my ears.

His laughter, which is contagious, instantly washes away any anger that's appeared. Through water spotted glasses I watch as his chuckles die, but his mouth remains open. The tip of his tongue touches his top lip almost as if pausing his voice.

Jamie leans over and shoves him. "In you go too Casanova."

There's another huge splash followed with him popping back up right in front of me. With his hands glued to my hips he presses his wet forehead against mine. "Totally worth it."

He inches his lips forward but the action is quickly ceased by the splashing of water on our faces.

That's right. Water blocked. That's a new one for me.

We turn to see Spencer swimming beside us with Jamie still on the edge.

Destin pulls me in closer, but let's the kiss moment go. Casually he suggests, "Water volleyball?"

"That's my shit!" Jamie exclaims before jumping in.

Hours pass faster than they ever have bringing us into the early evening. The day has been a dream come true. While it wasn't filled with hearts or flowers, I've laughed more times than I thought possible and for the first time in a long time, felt like I'm not playing second best to anyone.

Leaning so my back is against Destin's chest, I let out a satisfied smile that's short lived.

"I assume you're coming to the event," Spencer grumbles, lowering his beer bottle.

Destin casually replies, "What event?"

With a smug smirk Spencer comments. "Huh. She didn't invite you. Guess your date's almost over then."

No, he doesn't handle me dating very well, but to be fair I haven't done it much since he's been around. Yes, by much, I mean I've only been on one date in the last two years.

Before he can make the situation any worse, I turn over my shoulder. "I didn't invite you because I didn't think you'd wanna come."

"You gonna be there?"

"Of course. I kinda have to be."

"I wanna be wherever you are," Destin says sweetly.

His eyes light up and I feel my own do the same. "Really?"

"Absolutely."

Just as his lips lower in an attempt to touch mine, Spencer mumbles, "Awesome..."

Instead of kissing me he nudges my nose with his before peering around me at Spencer. "I get the feeling you don't like me very much dude."

"He doesn't like anyone who gets that close to Azura's face," Jamie inserts on a loud sigh. "Don't feel special."

Destin's eyes fall back into mine. "Well that makes two things we have in common." A small whimper comes out of me. "Ya feel me?"

I whisper, "I do."

"Good," he whispers in return.

Spencer breaks up the moment once more. "Shouldn't you be changing?"

Remind me to stay as far away from him at the event as possible. If I miss another chance to get kissed because of him, there's a chance I might try to drown him.

"Right." Shaking my head I prepare to get up. "I guess I should go get our clothes out of the backseat."

"I'll go," Destin volunteers. "Just grab your whole bag?"

"The red one, not the black one."

His interest is clearly peaked. "What's in the black one?"

"Whips, chains, handcuffs," Jamie mutters beside me. "Nothing for you."

"There better not be," Spencer grunts.

"That's fine." Destin shrugs taking my keys from me. "We'll just use mine instead." There's a small gasp that I can only assume is from Spencer. "Be back."

While we watch Destin head towards the exit, Jamie comments, "Shouldn't you be changing too Spence?"

"Probably," he mumbles and rises to his feet. "Look Azura-"

"Save yourself the embarrassment and get to moving," Jamie insists. He grumbles something but walks away leaving the two of us our first minute alone. "Now that we can breathe something other than testosterone I just wanna say, you did good."

Biting back a smile I ask, "Yeah?"

"Oh yeah. But here's my warning." Our faces turn to look at each other. "Be careful. While I would rather punch myself in the face than agree with Spencer out loud, Destin does have the whole tatted, playboy thing. He flirts like it's a profession. He's been eye fucking you all night like there's only one thing on his mind. If it's on yours too, great. If it's not, well...be careful because dudes like that have a way of changing a girl's mind."

Look, I'm not a complete idiot. I know she's right. He is a McCoy. That's what they're known best for. Fucking and forgetting. Tell me. Is it wrong to hope there's more there? That there's more to him? With everything else that's surrounding him, something inside me says that maybe what the world sees is nothing more than what they want too, not what's really there. What about you? What do you see?

**

"The docks," Destin says, glancing out his window. "Should I be worried you're gonna cut off my skin and turn me into a lampshade?" When I giggle he adds, "I'm pretty sure I would make a better suit."

Rolling my eyes, I take a right driving us past one of the storage units that constantly has a limo parked outside of it.

71

What kind of person rolls around in a limo, yet spends that much time at the docks?

Destin types away on his phone yet again spurring me to ask, "Is it another girl?"

He pauses very briefly. "Excuse me?"

"The reason you're constantly on your phone," I retort, pulling into a parking space. "Is it a girl you're seeing?"

Once he's finished typing he slides it back in his pocket. "It's my other job."

Confused I snap, "I thought you were just a mechanic."

"I thought you were just a bartender." Seeing his point I nod. "Azura, I know my brothers and I have a reputation, but for a sec, just one, can you forget about it?" My head hits the back of my seat while my eyes stare into his. "Remember the day in the bar you pointed out the differences in the three of us?"

"Yeah."

"Well one major thing you didn't point out, because you didn't know yet, is I don't sleep around like they did. That's not to say I haven't had my fair share of girls, it just means...I'm not cycling through them like tissues in cold season." My face twitches a smile. "I wanted what my parents had long before Merrick ever did. Long before Drew fell in love-"

"Drew's in love?"

"Yeah." There's a bitter-sweetness to the expression on his face. "And honestly, I don't wanna keep going like we were. After Ben...Merrick...and now Daniel's deaths, I realized I don't wanna die never knowing what that feels like. Maybe that makes me a giant pussy-"

"Or a giant romantic."

"Isn't that the same thing?" My laughter spurs his. "I'm just saying, drop the McCoy from my name and just give me a chance to be Destin." His tongue wets the lips I can't wait to have on mine. "Please."

On a light sigh, I whisper, "Okay."

"Okay," he comments back.

The two of us get out and I grab my black shoulder bag from the backseat. He slides his hand with mine and follows me towards the building where one single man is waiting, leaned against the building.

When we arrive in front of him, he lifts his eyebrows at me. "Code?"

I hold out my hand and insist Destin does the same. The guard looks both directions before taking out his black light flashlight. Seeing the symbol we were supposed to draw on to be admitted in, he pushes a button on a remote in his pocket. The door creeps open allowing us access.

"Where the hell are we going?" he whispers in my ear.

"You'll see."

At the end of the long hallway we're leaked into an oversized area where there are ramps for skateboarders who are already in motion, BMXers performing minor stunts, break dancers, girls dancing on each other, and people drinking while watching all of the various activities in awe.

"Skateboarding?" Destin questions over my shoulder.

I nod my head to the left. "That way."

We maneuver our way around, several guys and girls excited at my presence, glasses being raised at me, cat calls coming at such a rapid rate, Destin grips my hand tighter.

Most of the time no one notices me. However, here? I'm kinda a big deal. Almost like the Steven Speilberg or Michael Bay of underground events. Outside of them of course no one cares, but for the minor moments I record, a small flicker of belonging exists.

Finally, we exit out the side door where there's a smaller crowd gathered around. One of the guys with his board tucked under his arm, shouts out my name. "Azura!"

The rest cheer at my arrival.

Destin whispers in my ear, "Are you queen of something and haven't told me?"

After giving him a playful elbow, I acknowledge the skateboarders approaching me. "You ready to do this?"

Cage winks. "Just waiting on you."

Caleb his younger brother adds, "Are you ready?"

"Yup. Just give me one sec to set up. You can tell Cash to get the shit rolling," I instruct placing the bag on the ground.

They walk off and Destin grumps, "Am I gonna have to beat the shit out of a lotta guys to drive the point home you're taken?"

My breath hitches as I stand back up with my camera. "T-t-taken?"

Realizing what he said causes him to nervously scratch the back of his neck. "Uh...well...maybe?"

"Maybe?"

"Yeah?"

"Yeah?"

"Yeah." Destin clears his throat. "Taken."

I smirk to myself and turn to face where the show will start. Once my camera is ready to roll, I repeat, "Taken."

Music switches from pop to hip hop just as the lights switch from regular to black. Suddenly the entire outside of the dock is glowing in bright neon colors. The skateboarders who are waiting to be filmed are glowing and so are their boards. People cheer and I hit record making sure to capture the hyped up painted crowd before the stunts even start. Turning the camera towards the skaters I zoom in prepping to move along with them. Typical jumps off ramps kick off the show but within just a couple minutes, the more extreme adventures begin. Skaters perform tricks making sure to feed the crowd what they crave. Caleb and Cage, the stars I'm here to record grind their boards along the dock railing, flipping their boards and switching them before jumping off.

"Holy shit!" Destin shouts beside me. "Did you see that!"

Smiling I continue to follow them as they skate in unison into one handed hand stands revealing the bottom of their boards which are painted to go together. Cage's says X while his brother's says Treme. The trick gets wild cheers including very loud ones from my date.

When the show finally wraps up, I put my video recording camera away, to quickly grab the one for the photos. I take photo after photo, falling in love with the hobby I know may never take me any further than this with each click.

Sure, I like to record and cut videos, but there's a high chance I'll be stuck at underground gigs like this for a lifetime. Is that so bad?

Unsure of how long I've been taking pictures, I'm a little stunned at the feeling of Destin's hands slipping around my waist. Gently letting go of my camera to dangle around my neck, I enjoy the unexpected embrace.

Suddenly his face is lightly feathering the crook of my neck. In a very gentle voice he says, "Thank you for this, Azura. I needed it." With my heart skipping beats, I tilt my face upward to look at him. "And I don't just mean the escape from the sympathetic bullshit."

Destin doesn't wait for me to respond before dropping his mouth onto mine.

Let's be fair. Every time we hesitate we get interrupted!

The light pressure is enough to weaken my knees. As a soft whimper escapes, his fingers dig deeper into my skin holding me tighter than before. Our lips part cautiously, a nervous energy vibrating between us. The second his piercing strokes my tongue a hunger is unleashed. All of a sudden my tongue loses the restraint it had and attempts to devour him with no remorse. A small growl darts out of him while he rolls his tongue around mine, surrendering everything I'm begging for. My hand stretches up and grips the back of his head in fear of this moment ending.

78

I don't want it to ever end and I don't just mean the kiss.

Destin

I do not look like the cat that ate the canary. That's a stupid phrase anyway. Have you ever seen a cat eat a bird? They don't smile. They look fat, full, and pleased. Is it weird Daniel used to have a similar face after he got laid in the middle of the day?

Skimming the recently filed work orders, I'm surprised when the computer screen freezes. Before I have a chance to do anything about it, a face I hate appears on it.

Remind me not to punch the screen. He can't feel it.

"Ah. The geeky McCoy. Just the man I knew I wanted to have a word with."

"How'd you get on my screen?"

The Devil leans back in his chair. "You think you're the only one who knows how to hack into a system? Speaking of, that's what I'm here to discuss."

Pleased at the progress I've been making, despite Madden's command for me to stop, I smirk. "You don't enjoy being hunted like the wild animal you are?"

"Tsk, tsk." The Devil waves his finger at me. "Bad manners to speak to the man who could destroy the things you love with the snap of a finger."

"You don't have as much power as you think you do," I state bravely. After glancing out the office window at my family, I shake my head. "Especially not after I turned your license plate over to the cops last night on an anonymous tip."

Azura took me to the docks yesterday for this amazing underground show. Just so happens, I saw The Devil getting into a limo. I snapped a picture, reported it to the Commissioner. Even one less safe getaway from The Devil is a win.

"Hey, how'd it feel when they raided your spot? Find anything good?" The Devil clicks his fingers on his desk. "They find the cop's blood you've been shedding or evidence from any of your other savage tantrums?"

He smiles softly. "You get one warning McCoy. You and your smug as fuck brothers seem to keep forgetting it's me who gets to be judge and executioner. Try to be a smart boy before it gets you or that lovely little piece of ass that just pulled up dead."

My eyes flicker to see Azura climbing out of her car.

"Enjoy your day McCoy."

His face disappears off the screen and I instantly rush out of the office. Instead of looking smooth, I trip over a tool and nearly face plant.

Damn it! Don't laugh.

"Down boy," Knox mutters sliding out from underneath a Lexus. "We know she's yours."

Drew laughs as he wipes his hands. "You don't have to pee on her or anything."

"You're into that?" Wrench, the latest addition to our family closes the hood of the car he was working on. He scratches the back of his neck. "Is she?"

An awkward feeling flushes over me.

I've never been this fucking uncomfortable with sex jokes. Why do I suddenly wanna tell everyone to shut the fuck up and mind their damn business? Is this normal? What! I told you I haven't dated in a while...by a while I may have meant in um...years. What did we discuss already about judging?

"Hey everyone," Azura softly says, pushing her wavy hair behind her ear. "Morning..."

I smile and shove my hands into my pockets. She smiles wider and a shrug comes out of me. When her smile gets brighter, I bite my bottom lip to stop myself from pinning her against the work station and shoving my tongue back down her throat.

Best fucking kiss of my life last night.

"Apparently my brother's broken," Drew says tossing an arm around my neck. "So I'll say it for him. Good morning."

Elbowing him off of me, I say, "Hi..."

"Hi," she coos back.

Everyone in the shop has stopped what they're doing to watch.

This can't get any more awkward.

"Are you telepathically having sex?" Knox questions bluntly.

I was wrong.

Azura blushes and buries her face down. "No. I-I..I just...I brought breakfast tacos for um..."

"I heard tacos." Wrench walks over. "You said tacos, right?"

"Yeah Scooby. She's got Scooby snacks," Drew chuckles and folds his arms. "Question is, who are they for?"

Her face lifts again, much redder than before. "I um...I brought them for Destin, but I grabbed a few extra just in case you guys were hungry too."

That's my girl. Huh? Well you know what I mean.

"Thoughtful," Knox coos ushering her in with a wave. "Just don't do too many thoughtful things or they get spoiled and forget how to do simple things on their own like buy toilet paper."

"You get pissy when we buy the wrong kind," Madden grumbles, the only one still working.

"No one likes to wipe their ass with sandpaper."

Azura finds her way over to me and offers the bag. The moment her lips part, my tongue finds it's way inside her mouth not waiting for an invitation and disregarding the fact we are in a crowded work place.

Not subtle...I know. I know.

To my surprise she kisses back, the movement of her tongue causing my cock to stir.

Can't blame him for wanting to feel it too.

"You know the rule about action in the shop," Madden's stern voice pulls us apart. "We made that rule for Daniel but it's universal."

"Yeah," I comment back, my hand still on the side of her face. "I know..."

"She has tacos bro," Wrench whines.

Grabbing the bag I pass it to him and snake my arm around her waist. I turn to make introductions, "Azura, this is Wrench. Newest member of McCoy's Mechanics. He used to go to school with Madden."

Not the brightest, but having him around is almost like having a combination of Ben and Daniel all rolled into one. I think it's something even Madden needs to have around. In a way, I think we all do and not just because he's a fucking guru under the hood of any type of vehicle.

"My brother's you know," I continue as they all greet her. "Have you met Knox?"

"Once or twice." Azura nods. "Which reminds me, Knox my sister Angela said she was wondering how you liked that new French style lingerie store in the mall?" On a mumble she adds, "Though more stated that I ask than request the information."

Wrench who is half way done with his breakfast taco, questions with a mouth full, "You were in a lingerie store? What'd you buy?"

Unable to resist poking the bear I join in, "Who'd you buy it for?"

"Thigh highs?" Drew chimes in grabbing a taco from the bag. "Maybe one of those things that push a girl tits real high."

"That's called a corset asshole," she sighs. Turning to Azura she says, "Tell Angela it's cheaper to get it online from this place called Sal's."

"How do you know that?" Wrench shoves the remaining taco in his mouth. "Better yet can I see it?"

Madden slams his tool down.

Knox and Madden are not by any means together. They should be. I'm sure one day they will be. Well, I hope they will. For now we're forced to be subjected to these moments. Neither of them do jealousy well. It was funny to watch when we were younger. It was like a live action sitcom with curse words. Not to say it's not hilarious now, it's just we can add to fuel the fire. Sure that's probably wrong, but so is the years of pent up sexual frustration that could choke hold an NFL player with it's pinky.

"No you can't see it," Madden growls. "And who the fuck are you buying lingerie for?"

"The man I keep in my dungeon," she sneers grabbing a taco from the bag.

"You're into that?" Wrench mindlessly asks. "Do you need a new volunteer?"

"He will beat you to death with your namesake," Drew tries to intervene.

87

Very casually, I back the two of us into the office where I close the door. Tempted to press her tightly against the glass and assault her with my tongue, once more I fight the urge. Instead I say, "Thanks for bringing us breakfast. I've never had a girl bring me breakfast before."

"It's kinda my favorite meal of the day," she confesses with a shrug. "Those are from my favorite breakfast taco place. The Devil's Horn."

Hearing his name tenses my frame. I do my best to push down the anxiety he caused seconds before she walked up. "I can't wait to try one. You bought breakfast so dinners on me."

A disappointed look crawls on her face. "I have to work tonight."

"It's Sunday."

"The shops open."

"Not exactly. We're technically closed, but doing work. You at least close early?"

"We do."

88

"Then really late dinner it is." When she smiles I grab her hand and pull her closer to me. "Then I wanna show you something."

She gives me a skeptical look. "I don't sleep with guys on the second date."

"That's good. I don't sleep with guys on the second date either." Azura's head falls backwards in a fit of giggles. Letting the blissful feeling that's flooding me, control my lips I plant a kiss on the back of her hand. "You showed me a piece of you last night I didn't expect. I'm hoping to do the same."

"You already have," she coos, her head tilted upward. "But I'll always take more of Destin."

"Oh yeah?" I whisper lowering my lips again. "Prepared to overdose?"

"Go ahead and try..."

As if she's melted my ability to do anything else, I slam my mouth on top of hers. The frenzied action is followed by helping her onto the desk, our kiss never breaking. One hand anchors itself in her hair while the other slips underneath the back of her shirt, desperate to get even the slightest feel of her skin.

Fuck that shit is soft. Have I mentioned it's been a while for this too? The whole fucking kissing thing too. My brothers always assume when they got laid so did I, but fact is, it's been a long time. Do not ask how long. That's rude.

Captivated by the feel of her hands that have slipped under the front of my shirt, I prepare to yank the damn thing off when there's a banging on the glass window. On a displeased groan, I look over to see Madden with a stern expression.

She giggles and drops her face against my chest. "I can't believe we were making out with an audience."

"Eh." I shrug it off. "I'm just pissed we have to stop." Her snicker is my signal to lift her face back up to mine. "I have to get back to work, but...dinner tonight when you get off."

"Text me where."

"Will do." Our lips briefly touch. "Let me walk you back out."

The day moves surprisingly fast even with The Devil's warning haunting me in the back of my head. After we close the shop, I spend a couple hours, hacking video footage of the interrogation rooms where the Commissioner has been wasting his time with men so low on The Devil's pay grade they barely even know what his face looks like, and leaving clues to indicate The Devil is not following Cayman Island bank protocols so they freeze those accounts as well. Sadly while the evening ticks away I still find myself watching the clock for when she gets off almost as intently as watching it for when new information on The Devil pops up.

A little before midnight, I'm sitting in a booth at The Box, a local diner we've relied heavily on for years.

Back when we were in high school we ate at this place so often they talked about renaming it after us. What can I say? They have the best hot wings you'll ever eat in your life.

Moving my pen faster, I add a few more waves to the hair.

"Is that supposed to be me?" Azura questions, flopping down across from me. "Because if so, I think you're over exaggerating how good I look."

I stop doodling and look up at her. "That's not possible." The second she blushes I drop the pen. Slowly I extend my hand to grab hers. "Hi..."

She links her fingers with mine. "Hi..."

Yeah, not the most thrilling conversation, but what do you want from me. Something about her just kinda turns my brain to mush. Hasn't that happened to you before?

"How was work?"

Azura shrugs as she opens her menu. "It was work. How was the shop?"

"It was the shop," I echo her response.

After a brief look at the menu she darts her head up. "You eat a lot?"

"Not as much as I used too," I sigh. "But yeah. Enough."

"Then I'll have whatever you're having."

"Good. We're having squirrel nut nachos."

Her eyes enlarge. Her jaw drops. Her fingers tighten. The sight of all three causes me to erupt into laughter, which is followed with her own laughter and mumbled complaints about what a dick move that was. At the end of it all she says, "Don't make me regret trusting you."

"Hard for you to trust?"

"Is it hard for you?"

The air in the restaurant seems to undulate taking my emotions with it. Uncomfortable, I whisper out, "Could you blame me if it was?"

Azura offers me a soft smile with a hand squeeze. "No. I couldn't."

Before I get the chance to say anything else, the waitress comes to take our order. Once she's gone, instead of returning to the intense conversation that was on the horizon, I switch focus.

"So you like my drawing?"

"Yeah. It's really good. I didn't know you could draw."

"I used to do it all the time. Most of the tattoos Triple D has I designed."

"Oh yeah? Which one is your favorite?"

"Easy," I announce and extend my arm.

Azura's eyes fall on the heart shape, which is made to look like the organ with its veins and valves. There are pulse lines coming out of it to make the letter M.

"It represents our mom. She was the heartbeat of the McCoys. There wasn't any sacrifice too big or too small to save one of us."

"How'd she die?"

With a crooked smile I look away from the tatt. "Giving birth to Merrick."

See what I mean about never being too big or too small?

Azura's fingers slowly drag themselves up and down my inner arm. "Tell me, what do you miss most about her?"

"Aside from her pancakes?" The remark makes us both smile. "When I was little, it didn't matter what I drew, she used to put it on the fridge and display it like it was worth a million fucking bucks. Ya know, even back then we were all the same. It was hard to tell who was who, but Mom knew. She knew the little things that

94

made us different. She knew it mattered more to me to have my picture on the fridge than it did to Drew or Daniel. I needed that pride. I needed to know something, anything made me special."

The strokes on my arm get even lighter. "Everything about you is special, Destin."

My face twitches a smile. "Oh yeah?"

"Yeah."

Swallowing the anxiety from feeling too much too fast, I joke, "And to think you haven't even seen me naked yet."

With a giggle she rolls her eyes and pops my arm.

"So filming? That's your thing?"

"More or less," she answers. "I would do it more if I could find a job that paid me too, but for now underground extreme sports pay just enough to keep the dream alive."

Make a note for me to ask some friends who might be able to help her with that.

"What lead you to film?"

All of sudden the warm smile that was gracing her beautiful face disappears. Prepared to take it all back, to run the other direction, to slip in a dirty joke to ease away the tension, I'm stopped when she explains, "I never wanna forget again."

Perplexed by the comment I merely tilt my head.

"My mom married Angela's dad when we were four almost five. I don't remember anything before that point. I don't even remember them dating. I don't remember anything about my real dad or what she was like before she got remarried. I don't remember anything about the house we left. My mom doesn't have old photos or videos or anything that captured those special milestones for me. It's like one day I just existed in a new life without an old one. So, when I could I started taking pictures of everything. Recording moments I knew people would wanna watch again and again. Eventually it lead me to wanna do film. Documentaries. Anything to record something memorable. Before I knew it though, I fell in love with recording extreme activities. Getting to be there when they do that ollie over a chair or the first time they do a kickflip over a flight of stairs or grind down an escalator-"

"That's a thing?" I bark out in shock.

She giggles and pushes her hair behind her ear. "It is. My point is, I like capturing those kinds of actions and awe moments. There's nothing better than grabbing those memories, those accomplishments on camera for someone to relive years from now."

Our plates of hot wings and fries are delivered at a perfect time. The sad yet excited glow to her face is confusing to the point I'm terrified I might say the wrong thing.

You know, I don't have as many memories with my mom as I wished I did, but at least I have someone. I have bits from my early childhood, I can't imagine what it's like to have none. I also can't imagine what it's like to walk the halls of my house and not see my photo with my so called family.

After dinner filled with comic book talk, we stroll into the parking lot and over to my bike where I offer her a helmet. Immediately she shakes her head. "No way."

"Oh it's happening," I insist.

Azura shakes her head rapidly. "No way. No-huh. No. Nope. Not gonna do it." She attempts to hand me the helmet back. "No, Destin."

I slowly offer her a crooked smile.

"Don't give me that look. No. Bikes are dangerous. And scary. And loud. And-"

My arms are around her with my forehead pressed against hers. "And amazing. I'll protect you." Her big brown eyes plead with me. "I promise I'll always keep you safe."

Innocently she whispers, "That's a big promise."

"I know."

Her bottom lip slips between her teeth. Shaking away any final doubts she says, "Fine. Just this once."

"It only takes one ride to fall in love."

Azura softly asks, "With you or your bike?"

"I'm hoping both."

She smiles sweetly and gives in. "Alright Destin McCoy. I'm all yours."

God I fucking hope so.

Once we're both on my bike, I take us away from the diner, away from the lights and life of the busy city towards exactly what I promised to deliver. The curves in the roads cause Azura to grip me tighter. Her heart beat races against my back. Something about the amount of trust she has in me is soothing.

Rarely does anyone ever rely on me to do more than type on a keyboard. Hell even lately Madden's been second guessing if I can do that.

Off of the main winding road, we take a smaller two lane road until it leads us to the destination I planned. Parking my bike, I pull off my helmet just as the fall night wind kicks up.

Azura who is still gripping me tightly leans over my shoulder. "Can I take this off now?"

Chuckling, I nod and give her hands a pat to let go. As soon as we're both off with our helmets resting on my bike, I grab her hand, and pull her along the path until we reach the spot I'm dying to show her.

I wave my hand casually. "What do you think?"

She gives me a quick glance before she braces her hands on the railing of the bridge. "This is...this is incredible. Are those the city lights?"

"Yeah. Prettier from a distance aren't they?"

A small hum comes from her before she leans towards them. "They're beautiful." Quickly her face turns towards me. "Can I take a picture?"

"Of course."

Excited Azura pulls out her phone and snaps a few photos. Immediately after she insists we turn around and take a few selfies together.

Chicks and their selfies. I swear...

Once her appetite to capture this moment is satisfied she asks, "How do you know about this spot?"

My hands wrap around the railing. "Daniel found it."

Madden didn't always want us mixed up with The Devil. Hell, he tried to avoid letting us get tangled with it at all, but eventually he knew it was a lost cause. Eventually he accepted us into it, used our skills to harness better deals and more money in hopes of keeping Merrick far away from the survival traits we had developed. Needless to say that failed too.

"When we first got our licenses, we took random long trips all over the state, just 'cause we could. Pissed Madden off severely, but we needed a getaway. Daniel found this place and it became our in town road trip spot." I fold my hands together and rest my arms on the edge. "One time, while we were all here, avoiding the wrath of Mad Man Madden, Daniel convinced us all to get piercings. We argued for what felt like hours about what exactly to get. By the end of it, we decided we would all get something different, the first mark on our bodies of something to stand out."

"So that's why you got a tongue piercing?"

"Nah," I chuckle. "After that, at some point Drew let it slip what we had planned to do and Madden forbid us from doing it. So, the teen rebellion thing kicked in."

She snickers. "I am not surprised it did..."

"Our dad was in and out of prison, so Madden basically was our father most of the time. We hated his rules. His stupid rules, but as we got older we realized he did it to try to protect us."

"Protect you from what?"

More like who.

Instead of responding that way I move in closer. "Life. I'm learning we all do our best to protect the people we love in life." With her eyes now latched onto mine I confess, "I haven't been here since Merrick died."

Azura casually moves so our arms are touching. "Why'd you bring me?"

"Because you were brave enough to give me an escape when I needed it. I thought you deserved to see the one I used to have."

Her fingers link with mine, but her face turns to look back out across the water. Silence settles between us and for the first time in months, instead of hearing the faint echoes from the voices of the dead, there's a sweet serenity of stillness. I grip her hand tighter, thankful for it.

Eventually Azura and I talk a little more about my old memories with Daniel, Merrick and Ben, each one more freeing than the last. I haven't talked much about them since their deaths. It turns out the weight of the silence has been causing my chest to feel like it's about concave. However, every time I remember something about them, share what they were once like out loud, it seems one of those boulders is lifted. It makes me wonder if I keep Azura around will the weight of it all one day fade or at the very least be easier to carry.

The stroll back to Pepper is a quiet one. My arm is draped around her shoulder while her head is doing its best to stay pressed against me. When we arrive back at my bike, I turn her to face me. Her ass is slightly pressed against the seat and her head is lifted up in an inviting fashion. Gingerly, I push the hair behind her ear the way she likes. Unable to resist any longer, I place my lips on hers. On contact she sighs so softly that if I wasn't holding her I couldn't be certain it even fucking happened. The kiss starts soft and slow, my tongue showering hers with appreciation it's never given to anyone else before. Azura's hands grip the edge of my shirt sharply. This simple change ignites the pace to shift, which causes my tongue to do the same. Roughly I grab her hip with one hand, pleased when she whimpers again. Our tongues continue to entice one another, the game of who can bring who to their knees faster, a deliciously dirty one. Before I realize it, my mouth falls, anxious to taste more of her. My tongue trails itself down the side of her neck, the ball of my piercing acting as the best wing man ever.

It really fucking is.

"Destin," she whimpers, her nails digging into my skin from underneath my t-shirt.

Groaning, I switch hands to keep her neck where I want it while my other hand bravely travels south.

In a quiet voice she pants, "Destin...I...it's been a while since...well..."

My tongue strokes upward and she shudders.

Fuck I love that.

"Since what, baby?"

"Since anything," she admits as I roll my tongue around, finding a hot spot on her neck that parts her legs.

Pleased and thankful that the gate is open, I carefully slide my hand around to her inner thigh, the barrier of her tights still as sturdy as ever.

I hate these stupid things.

"Destin," her voice pleads though her hips rock towards me.

Sensing the apprehension as well as the arousal, I slip my lips off of the magic spot to look into her eyes. "If you say so no, I'll stop right now, put us on that bike and drive you back to your car, no questions asked."

Her hands fall from my body. "Is it just that easy for you? To just...walk away from me?"

"Fuck no," the words tumble out before I can put them in a tone that doesn't sound harsh. Clearing my throat I take a small breath and a step back. "But I'm not the dick that you secretly fear I am. I won't spout lines to get you into bed. I won't get you drunk to better the odds and I'll never fucking push you to do something you don't want to." The two of us hold each other's eyes hostage with our own. Something inside of me pushes me closer to her knowing the right thing here is not what my dick is demanding. "I should um...I should take you back to your car. It's late and-" is where the thought ends thanks to Azura's mouth back, desperate against mine.

Thank fuck...I'm not sure I can handle the idea of just double clicking a mouse anymore.

It only takes a few minutes before I've got her back in the position I pulled away from, except this time when my hand roams towards her pussy, she doesn't stop, she doesn't object, she simply stops breathing as she waits for my touch. My fingers slowly rub her

105

on the outside of her tights. Her teeth capture my bottom lip. Eagerly she begs, "More..."

Happy to oblige, I pull back, this time planting my hand on the edges of the article of clothing I hate.

That's right. To the dude or chick who invented this cock block clothing known as tights: Shame on you! Just fucking shame.

Azura slides off the flats she's wearing and lets me remove the stretchy leg covering material as well as her thong. On my way back up, my lips get a mind of their own, delivering a long deliberate lick up from her knee to the edge of her jean skirt. She feeds me a shudder and the desire to feast on them spurs my next action. With one good tug, I move her skirt up, toss her leg over my shoulder, and suck in a delicious mouthful of her sweet pussy. A sharp cry escapes, which barely registers. My tongue leisurely laps up the sticky sensation flooding from her. Each lick is long and dripping with devotion, determination to prove that this isn't about conquering her so much as surrendering myself. Relentlessly my tongue twist and turns. I indulge past the point of no return, every stroke refusing to miss the simplest of drop. On another satisfying mouthful, I use both my hands to grip her bare ass, needing her to stay at my mercy.

Suddenly her unsteady breath grabs my attention. "Oh my God, Destin...I'm gonna- I'm gonna-"

The ball of my tongue ring applies the necessary pressure against her clit, detonating her orgasm like a little red button I wasn't supposed to push. Her body becomes tumultuous and her voice frantic as it screams my name to the high heavens.

I hope someone up there is listening, because you can bet your ass tonight I'll be sending my thanks up for this girl.

Azura

Destin shoves the remaining slice of pizza in his mouth before he checks his phone for the sixth time.

That's right. I've been counting. He says it's another job and I believe him. Does that make me an idiot? Why would he lie to me though?

"Let me get this straight." He finally puts it down and wipes his greasy fingertips on his jeans. "*You* can actually skateboard."

"I can't fly over stairs and shit, but yeah. I can stay on my board," I explain. Skeptical his head tilts at me. "You wanna see me do a trick don't you?"

"At least one," he chuckles. "Show me you're not full of shit."

"Ugh," I grunt handing him the crust of my slice. "Fine. But you only get one."

"How would you feel if I said that to you?"

The comment causes my face to burst into flames.

He has this thing where any time he makes me come with his fingers he then has to make me come with his mouth. It's some weird rule he invented...at least I think he invented it. Did he? That's not a real thing right?

Destin chortles again, this time with the crust of my pizza hanging out of his mouth. "I love when you're speechless."

"Oh, you're just the worst..." Standing up, I grab my board and proceed to show him a small trick. It's nothing fancy, just a simple ollie to prove I'm not lying. When I roll back over, I toss a hand in the air. "See."

"Huh." He nods. "I would've never guessed in a million years you could skateboard."

With a smile I kick my board up and catch it, the trick making him nod impressed further. "Well that's why you should never assume anything."

"Where'd you learn to skate?"

"A group of friends in middle school. Learned a little more in high school. It was my go to sport when I wanted to get physical, but with glasses it's not the ideal one."

"I love your glasses," Destin immediately comments. "Do not get rid of them."

"I'm stuck with them," I innocently giggle.

"Can Angela skate?"

"No. She was good at your more traditional sports like volleyball. However, she loved hooking up with my skateboarding friends if they ever came over to the house. Insisted they could rotate their hips in ways football players couldn't. Or at least that was the gossip. Not real sure if she actually said that or not. She's never really talked to me much."

Destin's face scrunches as he pulls his knees to his chest. "Did you hook up with any of them?"

Nonchalantly, I shake my head. "They weren't really my type."

"What's your type?"

"Tall, dark, and tatted," I flirt.

"Damn right it is." He wiggles his eyebrows. After I giggle he asks, "So you and Angela weren't close at all growing up?"

"Nope." A shrug escapes me. "Different interests. Different hobbies. Most of the time it felt like we were co-existing rather than siblings. Honestly? I share a similar relationship with my parents."

A sad look comes across his face. "Didn't that bother you?"

"It used to when I was younger. It's hard enough having parents who aren't ever around, but it's even harder having a sibling not even acknowledge you exist. As I grew up, I accepted it for what it was. I had a house but not a home."

Destin lets out a long deep exhale. "I can't imagine what it would be like to grow up *not* close to my brothers. To not have family."

"It's a little different for you. You were triplets. Triple D to be exact."

He offers me a slightly broken smile.

Shit...I shouldn't have said that.

111

Before I can undo the solemn vibe I've created Cage appears over my shoulder. "Hey you."

"Cage," I greet him warmly turning for a hug. He squeezes me tightly and I swear I hear a small growl.

Did you hear that too?

"Cage meet Destin. Destin this is Cage," I introduce.

Casually he states, "I'm the boyfriend in the making."

Cage laughs and extends his knuckles for a fist bump. "I gotcha bro. No worries from this side. Things between Az and I are mostly business."

"Can we make it all business?" he questions.

"Destin!"

Cage laughs and fist bumps him again. "It's cas' bro. She films most of the videos for me and younger bro. We're hoping to pick up some sponsors attention and get put in one of the major games. Speaking of." He turns back to me. "Couple weeks, huge event down at Melly Fare Park. I'll get you the exact date tonight.

Gonna be a hot spot for sponsors. Can I count you in to come record?"

"Usual price?"

"I can swing a little more if necessary. We got a date?"

"We've got a date."

"Just to be clear, this is a skateboarding thing right?" Destin clears his throat, the frustration wrinkles on his face poorly hidden.

He's jealous and that's adorable!

"Yeah bro," Cage quickly replies. "You can come too. More support the better. I gotta get goin'. Caleb wants to whine about some trick he can't get tight. Az, I'll be in touch." He fist bumps Destin again. "D man keep our favorite girl happy."

Cage hops on his board and takes himself away.

"D Man?" Destin repeats. "That's fucking weird."

Giggling I face him. "Is it?"

"It's Triple D."

"Well he doesn't know that."

"Well maybe he should," he grumbles adjusting his folded legs again.

I roll my eyes. "I'll correct him next time."

There's a small pause before Destin says, "I passed some of your video links and photos to a few guys I know who might be able to get you a job doing that kind of thing in the big leagues."

Shocked, my jaw drops. "Seriously?"

"Nothing has come up yet, but yeah. The words out. Everyone agrees that you've got just as much talent off screen as they do on it."

A warm feeling spreads through me. Uncertain of the last time someone, anyone cared enough to go the extra mile for me like that, I sniffle away the instinct to cry. "Why don't you hop on my board and see what you're made of?"

"Are you kidding?" His eyebrows dart down. "In front of all these people you want me to look like an idiot?"

Playfully, I nod. "Yeah kinda."

With a good laugh, he hops up and shakes his head. "Fine. But you're kissing better any bumps and bruises I get."

I lean up on the tips of my toes to swipe at his bottom lip with my tongue. "Better make them good ones then..."

Destin groans and bites the spot I just tasted.

While yes, he has been generous over the last few days, I haven't gotten to return the favor. Yet. I'm going to change that as soon as I can. Believe me on that one.

Over the next hour or so, I demonstrate the basics, which within themselves are a disaster worth laughing over time and time again. Destin does his best, but continuously falls or trips. None of the injuries are a big deal, but I keep my word and kiss him or the area he demands every time. It reminds me of what I picture learning to ride a bike looks like. Eventually he gets some good speed and distance going. Like expected, he gets over confident and tumbles off the board into a gathering of bushes. After making sure I have his phone and my keys, I hustle over to see the damage that's been done.

Pushing my way around through the bushes to the center of the protected area, I see Destin lying flat on his back.

"You okay?"

He lifts himself up to rest on his palms. "I looked like a moron."

"You looked like a newbie."

"Well this newbie now has a few scrapes and bruises that need to be kissed again." He beckons me closer with a nod of his head. "Come here."

Slowly I crawl over to him until our lips are nudging yet not touching. His warm breath against my mouth elicits the softest moans. When his tongue snakes out to stroke my top lip, I pounce incapable of withstanding the building friction.

Let me see you try.

Rapidly moving, our teeth gnash in a fit of out of control kisses and bites. Enamored with the fevered chaos the slightest physical connection creates, I kiss him harsher, pulling him into me by his shirt. Destin groans his compliance, his own hands yanking me closer by my belt loops. The two of us tumble backwards, my body straddling his. With one of his hands tangled in my hair and the other on my ass, I moan loudly. Our hips rock together the simulation of what's to come sooner rather than later enough to tempt me to throw out the idea of waiting any longer.

I'm trying not to be that girl, *but he's making it really hard.*

Pulling my lips off his, I drag them over to give his neck a bite as my body slips off to lie beside him.

A groan creeps out alongside my name, "Azura..."

Excited by the sound of my name, I give his neck another suck, this time letting my hand slide down his chest with one determination in mind. Soft whispers and grumbles continue to fall out of him, until I find success.

The second my hand wraps around his cock he loudly groans, "Fuck...."

"Shhh," I whisper in his ear. "We don't wanna get caught."

I repeat the stroke, the constriction of the situation obviously frustrating to both of us. Destin adjusts until he frees his cock from the jean prison it was suffering in. With a bit of nervousness as well as elation, I relocate my body between his legs, and capture the recently sprung prisoner with my mouth.

"Fuck!" He calls out so loudly, I let go. "Wh-"

My hand tightens over his mouth. In a whisper I scold, "I wanna keep going, but you have to be a little more quiet. Okay?"

His beautiful toffee eyes that are coated in euphoria plead loudly while his head simply nods. Removing my hand from his lips, I return mine to the taste I've been desperate to have. The second his cock is back against my tongue a strangled moan comes from him, vibrating my body with his. Drunk with exhilaration, I suck harder, lower my mouth further, each movement feeling like scraps being tossed to a starving animal. I begin to move voraciously with the inability to mollify the craving that's coursing through my blood and pooling between my thighs. Somehow with every inch I take I become more insatiable, the flavor more deliriously delectable.

Destin's choked voice says, "Fuck..." There's more grumbles, but then he repeats, "Fuck."

When his fingers wind in my hair helping keep the bobbing of his cock at a pleasant pace for both of us, something inside of me snaps. Something calls to me to slide him in further.

Destin's dick stiffens at the change of depth just as his hand grips my hair tightly, "Fuck, I'm coming." Warm rush after warm rush fills my mouth at such a speed, my body that felt like it was

118

dying without his dick diving deep just seconds ago, actually reaches a level of contentment.

Slowly I deliver one final caress with my tongue before giving the spent organ it's final freedom. I wipe away any remaining proof of what occurred from the corners of my mouth and lift my head up, face glistening with bliss. A level of pride seeps into my system as I watch Destin struggle to lift his limp body up. When he finally does, his mouth opens flashing me his magical partner in crime, but he doesn't say anything.

With a light giggle I whisper out what is definitely my new favorite word, "Hi..."

He nods, wets his lips, and whispers back, "Fuckin' hi...."

So not the most impressive post orgasm conversation, but it could be worse right?

Destin

With one hand I scroll down my phone, pleased to see The Devil's helicopter has been confiscated and his pilot arrested.

Did I fail to mention I'm damn good at hacking?

I drop the device beside my leg and pick my pencil back up just as Azura turns her face away from the T.V. "What do you think of this one?"

She hums, "I think that would look badass on my board." Her compliment makes me smile, but it's short lived. "However, I'd settle for you on your phone less."

A sigh comes from me as I shade Super Mario's hat.

When she asked me to create a new doodle for her board I decided I needed to sharpen my skills with practice rounds. What started off as a favor became a perfect escape to the persistent thoughts of my brothers' deaths. It's like with each drawing a little stress is relieved and a small bit of peace is felt inside. Every time I'm with Azura there's a similar effect. That's good right?

Slightly annoyed I grumble, "I already told you it's not another girl."

"I get that." She sits up straight. "And I believe you, but Destin, I've been here for two hours and you've spent over half of it on the phone working."

"I know but-"

"It's cool," her voice whispers. "I should go anyway. I need to get to work. Are you still coming to Jamie's fight with me Friday night?"

"Of course."

"Okay. I guess I'll see you then."

Azura prepares to get up when my arm that's draped around her ceases the action. "Baby, wait."

There's a frustrated expression on her face when she turns to look at me. "What, Destin? You're busy and I need to get to work."

Seeing the hurt in her eyes, I move the drawing notebook and phone onto my nightstand.

Don't worry. It's bottle free. Don't ask if my computer's porn free. That's neither here nor there.

"I'm sorry," I apologize. "I'm not used to anything besides my computer needing that much attention-"

"So now I'm needy?"

"That didn't come out right," I rush to fix this conversation. "I meant, most of my life has revolved around work and the computer, so can you just...bear with me as I adjust to having something this amazing in life?"

A hint of a smile finds its way on her face. "Did you just call me amazing?"

Relieved, I nod. "I did. There's not a single part of you that isn't." Before she can say anything else I lean over giving her neck a soft kiss. Instantly she lets out a copious breath and sinks her body against me. My tongue rolls around in languorous circles, the ball of the ring teasing the spot on her neck that turns her into putty. I drag it up until I captures her earlobe, sucking until her body is ready to submit to anything I ask.

"Destin," she whimpers. "I...I...I have to get to work."

After giving her lobe another hard suck I counter, "So do I."

A light whimper seeps out just as my fingers runs across her boob, her nipple hardening from the feathering. Giving it a little tug seems to make the soft cries get loud. My cock bumps against my jeans ready for action unaware of the fact now's not his turn. I slide my fingers over to the other side repeating the action. This time the withering gets more intense. Entranced by the sight of her this turned on by me, I drop my mouth back to her neck. Desperate for more moans to echo around my room, I slide my hand down her side towards my newest addiction. Grateful she is a fan of jean skirts for work, I slip my finger underneath her thong. Immediately I groan, appeased with the pleasant warm welcoming my fingers receive.

Azura arches her body at the intrusion, my name falling off her tongue like a last request. "Destin..."

With a little bit of help, I manage to move her skirt all the way up and my two fingers deeper inside. Her breathing hitches as she bites down on her bottom lip to stop from screaming.

"It's okay, baby," I insist, anxious to hear the sound of my name again. "Scream...Let the world know who's claiming this pussy."

Suddenly her muscles clamp down on my fingers, demanding they do just that. Azura lets out a louder moan. My teeth nip at her neck while I pump ferociously, some unfamiliar nature clawing at me to tear an orgasm out of her. The increased speed and attention on her clit has her trembling, helplessly begging for more yet pleading she can't take it. The need to hear her orgasmic screams reaches higher altitudes, which is when the nipping of her neck turns to sharp sucks and the motion of my fingers turns to a rocking one that creates a round of rife moans.

On a sharp gasp, a rhapsodic cry comes from her. "Oh my god, I'm coming!"

Azura lets go. I still my finger absorbing severe shock wave after shock wave, my own cock seconds from leaking in my jeans.

That would be embarrassing as fuck.

After releasing her neck that I've marked, I let my head simply fall against hers. A small smile crawls on my face.

Maybe not working all the time isn't such a bad thing. Someone wanting and needing me in the present has much bigger and much more beautiful benefits than waiting for revenge to kick into full effect. I didn't think I'd want anything as much as I did that, but I'm starting to think I was wrong. It's one error I'm okay with.

Azura

"Jamie typically win these things?" Destin asks as he pays our cover charge to get in.

I tried to pay! I swear! He has this weird thing where he hates if I pay. He insists I save my money for something I really want, but what I really want money can't buy and now more importantly, I already have it. Oh...I did not mean to go paperback romance novel on you. Sorry.

The door is opened for us at the same time I refresh his memory. "Do you remember how beautiful her face was?"

"I remember how beautiful your face was that day," he says, shoving his wallet back in his pocket. "And every day since."

His compliment is rewarded with a peck on the cheek. "Jamie's undefeated at the moment. She doesn't like her face hit-"

"She's in the wrong sport," Destin chuckles.

We make our way around the crowd towards the bar.

"You would think," I giggle back. "My point is, she doesn't like to be hit in the face and the only way to prevent that is to knock her opponent the fuck out faster. This is her 10th fight this year."

"She wanna go pro?"

"There's talk," I reply with a shrug. "But I don't know."

"She should not go pro," a voice says from beside us. Quickly our faces turn to see one we both know well. "I make too much money off of her underground."

"Vinnie!" Destin calls out giving him the manly half hand shake, half hug.

What is that thing called? Does it even have a name? Let's call it the man pat. Or the bro hug. Huh? Oh Vinnie! Vinnie is like an underground betting guru. He's got his hands in anything that he can make a profit from. He's a sweet guy for the most part. I know him from these things and his trips to the bar with his girlfriends. Destin's brothers and cousin used to race for him. Not real sure if they do anymore.

Destin's arm falls around my shoulder. "What the fuck are you doing in this place?"

"I just told you." He pushes up his black box frame glasses, which are similar to my own. "Rock 'em, Sock 'em makes me a lot of money."

Destin's confusion makes me giggle. "Rock 'em, Sock 'em?"

"Jamie's nickname," I answer as we move closer to getting a drink order.

"What kinda fucking name is that?"

Vinnie moves with us. "Dude, you remember Rock 'em, Sock 'em Robots?"

"Of course. Daniel stole the neighbor kid's so we could play."

Why doesn't that surprise me?

"Let's just say, when she hits, it's for the face and typically lasts as long as that fucking game did. A couple punches is all it takes before her competition is knocked the fuck out." Vinnie describes. "Bank roll off of her."

"Damn," Destin mumbles.

"Hey." Vinnie nudges my arm. "I got your video portfolio passed to this dude I know who works for X-treme X-press-"

"The extreme games company? The one that hosts the biggest extreme sports across the world?"

"That'd be the one." He winks. "Turns out they liked what they saw and you should be getting an email any day now to set up a Skype interview."

Shock drops my jaw. "Shut up."

"Or..." Vinnie tilts his head at the bartender. "I could buy you two congratulations drinks instead."

"Oh my god!" I squeal and toss my arms around him. "This is amazing!"

Vinnie hugs me back at the same time he says, "Chill Triple D. It's just a hug. You're as bad as Merrick used to be."

"Yeah well, I now understand why his balls were always in a twist over his girl." He gently pulls me back towards him. "Happens when you fall for someone."

Unsure of what to do with either of the new pieces information I simply bob my mouth.

"Three shots of Kiss My Ass," Vinnie orders.

"On me!" I squeak reaching into my back jean pocket for my card.

"No fucking way," they say in unison.

Um...really?

"I'll pay." Destin grabs more cash from his pocket. "For yours too Vinnie."

He nods his appreciation while the male bartender gets to work. With admiration in my voice, I sigh at Vinnie, "I honestly can't thank you enough for this."

"Don't thank me too much. It was Triple D's doing. All I did was what was asked. He's the real hero here."

Feeling my body overflowing with joy and reverence, I turn to face my boyfriend who is beaming at me with a crooked smirk. Instead of expressing my gratitude with my words, I shove my mouth on his, showing appreciation with push after push of my tongue against his. An animalistic growl comes out of him as one of his hands pulls me closer to him by my ass.

"I hate to be a cock block," Vinnie starts. "Especially because it violates my own personal code of honor, but can you pay the man?"

Destin hums, gives my tongue one more tease, and pulls away. Casually he hands the bartender a fifty and insists he keeps the change. The three of us raise our glasses and he announces, "To things finally looking up in life."

"I'll fucking cheers to that," Vinnie agrees.

Clinking my glass with theirs I exclaim, "Mc too."

The shot smoothly runs down my throat tasting like chocolate milk.

Totally recommend it!

"I'll see you guys at the fight," Vinnie announces before strolling away.

"Want another?" Destin offers.

"Nope." I shake my head quickly. "I wanna be sober for what's next."

"The fight?"

I wink. "After..."

He bites his bottom lip at me and I giggle. Grabbing his arm, I pull him away from the bar, moving us towards the lower caged in area where we will be watching Jamie in just a few minutes.

The area is crowded, but we manage to make our way to the front. Once we're there Destin wraps his arms protectively around my waist. A small smile comes from me. Feeling secure, I lean back against him, even more cheerful when he kisses the side of my forehead.

Was that a fuck off kiss to everyone else? Are you smirking too?

Moments after we spot Vinnie across the room, the fighters take the ring. It's only a brief prelude before the two of them are exchanging blows. Much like Vinnie described, it barely counts as a fight. Jamie's opponent spends more time blocking than countering or actually making a move of her own. Like the champ she is, she wears the girl's defenses down until they drop. That's when she

131

unleashes swing after swing, each strike so sharp it causes me to grit my teeth. Watching the woman's face ruddy so quickly tenses my body. Destin gives my arms a consoling rub. Jamie's opponent falls to the ground, knocked out before my friend's broken a sweat.

Yeah. Always bet on Rock 'em, Sock 'em.

The announcer holds up Jamie's hand as she waves the other to encourage the boisterous crowd to get even louder. Destin and I cheer alongside, appreciating the small shout out nod she always gives to me when I show up.

I try to make as many of these as I can. It's usually not an issue, but shit happens.

After the announcer indicates the next round of fighters are about to take the ring, we move out of the main area and linger in the room with the bar waiting for Jamie. When she arrives we shower her with praise, make small talk for a bit, and cut out right after her date finds us.

Chicks love to see her knock another woman out. She gets the luckiest after she's gone a round. The next morning details are usually shared over my favorite breakfast tacos, but not this time. This time, I plan to be too busy with morning sex to make the meet up.

Destin and I head back to my house with him driving my car.

I'm not comfortable taking his motorcycle everywhere and he prefers to drive, so this makes everyone happy. It's not really that big of a deal anyway. I don't really like to drive.

As soon as we pull into the driveway he pulls out his phone. I bite back the immediate urge to snap about him working. Casually he mentions, "Just letting Madden know not to expect me home tonight."

Thankful I'm not about to share my night with work, I ask, "You have to check in?"

His head tilts and he hesitates before answering. "With...so many deaths so close together, it's a courtesy thing."

"Oh."

Now I feel like the world's biggest bitch.

Sweetly he looks up at me. "It's cool. You didn't know. Now you do."

133

The two of us get out together, hands linking up at their first available chance. He hands me my keys to open the door.

"You know my parents are still out of the country."

"Oh yeah?" Destin whispers over my shoulder, the door creaking open. "What about Angela?"

"A date." Turning around to face him as I back into the house I add, "She doesn't bring them home. It's one of her rules. Only special guys can come over."

With a crooked smirk, he locks the door behind him. "You mean to tell me, it's just you and me?" When I nod slowly he continues to stalk me down the hall towards my bedroom. "All night?"

"Most likely."

"Good." His voice seems a bit shaky. "Because it is my mission before morning for the entire fucking neighborhood to know my name."

I barely have time for another breath because he swiftly presses his lips to mine as he pushes me against the wall, rattling the pictures on it. Hungrily he consumes me, the pushing of his tongue

134

sucking the strength to stay upright from my body. In a vortex of sucks, nibbles, and licks, I'm swept away into an ecstasy that has my pussy soaking long before we reach the bed.

God, I hope it's not long before we reach the bed.

With a pull of his shirt, I start to move us back towards my room. The second we cross the threshold into it, he shuts the door with his foot, rips off his shirt, and stalks towards me. Feeling helpless in the sexiest way, I flop down on the edge of my mattress only to have his body blanket mine seconds later. Frenetic, our mouths demand each other's surrender, our tongues the fatal tools. Destin redirects his efforts momentarily to my neck before yanking my sweater over my head. As soon as he gets one glance of my bra, he undoes it. On a heated groan his pierced pleasure provider delivers the world's most tantalizing twirl around my nipples. With each tease, my pussy pulsates in objection it's not the one enjoying the fun. For what feels like hours, his mouth tours my body, the journey to my lower half the longest of my entire life. Once I'm completely naked and his hot breath is inches from delivering what my aching pussy is dying for, he pulls his body completely up.

In a huff I say, "Really?"

A playful smirk crosses his gorgeous lips. "Did you...did you want something?"

135

Just as I prepare to threaten the shit out of him, his pants drop revealing the only thing my pussy craves more than his tongue. Moaning my opposition as much as my desperation just makes him smile wider.

"That's what I thought," he whispers. His tongue wets his lips, but he remains still. "Before I do the thing I can't wait to fucking do, you should know I use EA."

EA which is the street name for a drug called Enilanerda. It's basically a miracle liquid. It ramps up your immune system to kill any STDs that may try to weasel their way in. One shot and you're practically stress free from the consequences of sex. It even helps protect from unwanted pregnancies. Two things I should mention. The first, it's illegal. My step dad has reasons stacked upon reasons why it should stay illegal, but I feel like as a pharmaceutical rep his opinion might be a bit biased. The other downside with EA is it has an effect on your body chemistry. Every time you take it, you run the risk of becoming dependent on it in order to get an erection or wet. You also run the risk as a dude never getting it up again and as a woman, we run the risk of becoming infertile. I don't judge to anyone who uses or doesn't. We all have to make our own choice, ya know?

"But it's been...a long time since I've had a need for it."

Curious I ask, "How long?"

"Um..." He scratches the back of his neck. "A little less than a year."

In disbelief I lift my eyebrows. "But I thought-"

"I'm really good at keeping up appearances," he confesses. "Besides, most of the reputation of being a McCoy does all the hard work for me." Seeing the slight anguish in his eyes he pleads, "I hope um...that doesn't change your mind."

With a sweet grin I shake my head. "Not at all. It's been longer for me."

"How long?"

Dreading my own response I whisper, "A little over three years."

Destin fights the urge to smile, the wheels in his head clearly turning.

Cockiness is cute and *obnoxious.*

"EA?"

"The pill," I inform. "My step dad would kill me if I even thought about EA."

"Works for me," he says softly before grabbing my legs, yanking me to the edge of the bed. With a sly smirk he advises, "You're gonna wanna hold on."

I grip the sheets with my hands as he positions my legs to be folded against my body. Passionately, but powerfully he pushes his cock inside, the immediate parting of my pussy painful enough to make me squirm in discomfort.

Destin releases a long deep exhale. "Relax, baby. I won't hurt you."

Shutting my eyes I do my best to melt into my sheets, the gentle rocking of his dick, swiftly moving from pain to pleasure. A deep panting begins as my pussy grips his cock, coaxing it to move deeper. His hands grip my legs firmly. He pulls me closer. The start of what was a gentle stroke now slamming so vigorously, so precisely he elicits cries of his name as if I'm afraid he won't remember it if I don't continue to remind him. Thrust after thrust trembles through my body. I struggle to open my eyes, to stare into the ones that are giving me something I've never experienced before, but can't. Lost in the tumbling tasty turmoil, I let my body remain trapped at his ruthless demands for an orgasm to come out of me.

Barely audible I whisper, "Des..."

"Fuck," he groans in return, fingers so tight I know it's going to bruise.

You should see the hickey he gave me earlier this week.

I beg, "Don't stop."

"No fucking way," he grumbles and pushes hard this time the bouncing action, forcing his cock to the hilt.

My hands ceaselessly claw at the sheets, desperate for stability, desperate for something to make the ecstasy stretch out longer than I know my pussy will allow. A defeated moan escapes just as my pussy begins to clamp down repeatedly on his dick. Waves of euphoria drown me while I verbally beg for more. On a low growl, Destin's body hunches forward, his own proof of pleasure overflowing the tight space. Our breaths continue to heave while fighting to keep every little scrap of air we can. Finally spent, he lowers my legs. His forehead hits mine.

When I open my eyes, he gives my bottom lip a lick. Sated he coos, "Hi..."

Dazed and delirious, I utter the only word back I'm now learning I need to. "Hi..."

Destin

I've been out of the sex game for a while. Quick question. Six times in one night....am I slacking? To be fair the final time was with the sun rising, but still, is that lower than I should be? Why is your jaw on the floor? Pick that up.

The feeling of a warm hand wrapped around my cock encourages my eyes to open. To my surprise, Azura is not only wide awake, but grinding her body against mine.

Groaning at the wake-up call, I prepare to pull her onto my lap when she shakes her head. "Not yet."

I open my mouth to object but am hushed by her tongue anxious to find mine.

Okay, so seven won't be so bad for getting back on the horse I guess.

Her stroking increases in speed, her fingers working in an unpredictable pattern of squeezes of my shaft and soft tugs of my balls. Something about the combination has me growling, impatient to get inside her again. Running my fingers through her tangled hair I give it a small tug. She retaliates by tugging my nuts. Another low roar ripples out and I find myself ready to come already. My dick stiffens almost as a warning of what's pending. At that point Azura straddles me and lowers herself slowly, insuring she coats every inch of my cock.

A helpless feeling pins me to the bed, my arms flopping backwards. "God you're amazing...."

She giggles, lifts herself off, and repeats the action this time her hands bracing themselves on my arms. Trapped in paradise, I let my eyes roll back into my head as her pussy grinds on top of me. Slowly she rocks her hips, discovering the spots that cause her to moan louder than others. I make mental notes to explore them again later. Struggling to hold back the nut I can't wait to bust, I stifle my groans behind gritted teeth. Azura stumbles upon a rhythm that seems to suck the breath right out of her. All at once a mixture of moans and mumbles of my name topple off her tongue until she screams out, "Destin!"

Her pussy vibrates on my dick, ripping apart any restraint I had left. The two of us come in tandem, pulse feeding pulse. My hands strain. A bellow bursts from deep inside and bounces throughout the house.

Azura collapses on top of me. With a crooked smile I sigh, "Good morning to you too."

Another giggle comes from her. She buries her face in my chest and wiggles her head back forth. When she finally looks up, there's a red shade I love more each time I see it. "I don't know what came over me....I've never done that before."

"Climbed on top?"

"That either," she mumbles.

Fist bump me for being lucky enough to be first for that shit.

"I meant just woke up a guy for sex."

"You have my blessing to wake me up any time, day or night for anything." She grins, so I add, "Especially sex."

After she chuckles and playfully swats at me she states, "I am going to get us breakfast."

"Alright. Let me get dressed."

"No," she coos. "*I'm* going to get us breakfast. You stay right here. In this bed. And wait for me naked."

"I don't see anything wrong with this plan," I laugh lightly. "But are you sure you don't want me to come with you?"

"Positive." Azura strokes the side of my face with her finger. "I wanna get you breakfast in bed. Let me?"

What kind of jackass denies a woman that? Hey, hey it was her idea!

"This time. Next time I get you breakfast."

"Deal." A light peck lands on my lips. "I'll be back before you know it."

Folding my arms behind my head, I watch as Azura covers up the gorgeous creation that is her body. If her caramel skin isn't enticing enough, the way her body curves from casual athletics, but constantly moving behind the bar is enough to drive any dude mad. Swirling my tongue around each and every spot is definitely high on my list of new favorite activities. Before she slips out of the room she gives me a small finger wave. The thought of grabbing my phone to do a bit of work runs out of my brain almost as soon as it runs in. Exhausted, I shut my eyes, the idea of catching a few more Zs before helping out in the shop today more tempting than anything else.

Well, almost more than anything else...

The feeling of my lap being straddled lifts my eyelids as well as a smile. However the sight on top of me shifts me from excited to panicked instantly.

"What the fuck are you doing?"

Angela wiggles. "I think your cock knows."

Willing my wake up wood down doesn't take much effort.

Apparently he doesn't like this surprise either.

"You look just like him," she whispers softly.

"Get up."

"I mean...just like him."

"Triplets," I remind her my hands moving to her hips to help her up. "Please get up."

Her hands grip mine, the robe she's wearing parting to expose her tits that are not as magnificent as her sister's but still a decent pair. "Do you fuck just like him too?"

145

Is it wrong I wanna say better? I mean I don't actually know, but a guy can hope he is the best in his family right?

"Angela," I state firmly. "Get up."

In a soft sob she begs, "Please. I need this..."

"I-"

"I miss him." Another sob comes from her. "I just wanna be with him one more time and say goodbye..."

Having a small inkling of what's that like I start, "I get that. I really do. But-"

A clashing of objects, shoots our attention to the doorway where Azura looks like I'm beginning to feel. Like the world is over before it even got started.

"Just let you be Destin?" She says slowly as Angela scampers off of me. "Mistake learned."

"Azura-"

"Don't." Her lifted hand clamps my mouth shut. "Get your shit and get the hell out of my house *McCoy*."

Angela tries, "Azura-"

"Out of my face," she snaps at her sister.

Struggling with the tie to her robe she disappears.

She is officially the worst sister in the world.

Immediately I try again, "Azura-"

"Do not make me repeat myself."

Frustrated, I hop out of bed, grab my clothes and slip them on as quick as possible. I twitch to say something else but that's when she turns and storms off. On my way out, I notice her grabbing the mop and broom, faint cries escaping her. Wanting to help, to fix this giant misunderstanding, I take a step in that direction.

When her eyes meet mine again, she sniffles. "Please, just go."

I nod. With a deep sigh I run my fingers across my forehead impressed at the speed my life seems to be making a habit of turning from golden to shit.

Check the World Record. Pretty sure you'll see my face there.

After a long ride around the city filled with a pit stop for gas and a bagel since I didn't get anything in me for breakfast, I park my bike next to Drew's. There's a small tug in my chest knowing that's where Daniel's bike used to be. Should be. Is supposed to be. Another grunt escapes me as I drop my helmet on my seat.

Entering through the garage I'm surprised to see it vacant of everyone except Wrench. Confused I toss my head at him. "Where the hell is everyone?"

"Mandatory family lunch meeting upstairs."

Immediately I pull out my phone to see the emergency texts from Madden to bring my ass home.

Great. This day is just gonna keep getting fucking worse.

"I was told to hold down the fort," he says before having another bite of his sandwich.

"So you annihilating a turkey club is you doing that?"

Wrench sucks dressing off his fingers. "It's a BLT man."

"That's what matters," I mumble and head for the staircase that's connected.

Quickly I rush up and inside to see my brothers and Knox gathered in front of the television I am beginning to loathe since it's sole purpose now seems to be a way for The Devil to communicate.

"Right. On. Time," he says, spotting me. "The man of the hour."

I slide my keys into my pocket and approach the backside of the couch where I drop my hands. "The most wanted man in America."

"Flattered." He waves a hand at me. Seconds later he has a bite from a slice of watermelon. "You know...you McCoys don't seem to fucking get it."

Drew who is sitting directly in front of me questions, "What's that?"

"Killing you off is simple." The words tense Madden who is located on the other couch beside Knox. Her hand clamps down on his thigh to keep him in place. "It's not even fun anymore." He sucks his teeth. "It was kind of fun in the beginning, now it's just sad..." On that note we all strain to stay still. "Problem is you're now becoming pests."

"Our turn to be flattered," Drew quips.

The Devil's eyes lock onto me. "At first it wasn't a big deal. So you closed a few bank accounts. Had a house taken here, a vacation home there. My plates tagged, ran, and followed. Warehouses shut down. Drug routes blocked. A man can live with that."

I smirk widely.

Damn right I'm proud. You see how rattled he is?

"But then you took it too far. Fuck with my money, fuck with my drugs, but never fuck with a man's plane!" Enraged he points the rind of the slice at me. "Never fuck with a man's ability to tour the skies!" He chucks the fruit and lifts his eyebrows at his tantrum. "My helicopter! Then my plane! Too far Geeky McCoy! Too fucking far!" His voice rises. "You wanna fucking play? You wanna see who has the bigger set of balls? My move, right?"

150

Swallowing my nerves, I answer, "Yeah."

"Good." The Devil tosses his hands in the air. "Because it's a brilliant one. Who here has a girlfriend in WITSEC?" Dread drops to my stomach. "Well it's not Drew because his girlfriend is dead."

The Devil thinks that and we are to keep it that way until he fucking is.

"You two aren't fucking, which is why she scowls like her vibrator probably does after a hard night and why you're just so....fucking...angry," he whines and makes pout faces at them. "So that means...."

Immediately I try to push down harder at the horror that's hauling itself through my system. "You're lying."

He bobs his head back and forth. "Am I?"

"I call bullshit."

"Oh..." The Devil nods. "Just one second." He makes a fake phone with his hand. "Hello Bullshit? Yes, you know me very well. Quick question, Destin's girlfriend Azura-" He abruptly stops his own voice. "Oh I need to call The Truth for confirmation? Of course.

Duh." Hanging up the pretend phone he mimics tossing it over his shoulder. "That's not enough to make you panic. This'll help. It's the BV MC who wants her."

A small gasp comes from Knox as my jaw trembles.

The BV MC stands for the Barbaric Viking Motorcycle Club. They conduct business quite similar to Vikings. Instead of raping, it's rough sex, pillaging is in the form of drugs and territory snatching. They have some fucked up code where honor is at the top. Brutal is the name of their game and explanations are rarely needed or provided.

The Devil smiles brightly. "Did I fail to mention they're on their way to kill her? Right...now. Oopsy. Eh well. You fucked with something I love. I'm returning the gesture." Terror floods my eyes and he winks at me. "Have a good day Geek McCoy."

Our screen goes black. At that very moment the instinct to let my legs buckle kicks in. The pressure that was once relieved from life bares back down with a vengeance. Before my knees have a chance to touch the floor, Drew swoops in bringing me back to my feet.

"No," he fusses. "Get up."

"I told you to stop fucking with him!" Madden shouts.

"I know," I meekly reply.

"You're so fucking hard headed!"

"I fucked up," my voice shakes. "I know. But Azura-"

"We're not doing this shit," Madden grouses. "We're not losing another fucking person."

"Madden-"

"Just fucking forget it! Fucking focus! Get your head in this!"

Barely able to breath, I nod my compliance.

"Where is she?"

"I-I-I don't know." Panic pushes out. "We- We- We had fight and I bailed."

"Of course you did," Knox grumbles. "The McCoy way. Things get too intense. You bail."

"Not now!" Madden snaps. He instructs with a firm point. "Triple D, check the bar. I'll check her house. Drew stay here and be on standby in case she or they show up here."

"I can check her house," Knox volunteers.

"No," Madden shuts her down.

"I can fucking help," she argues as he grabs his keys.

"I said no-"

"But-"

"Fuckin' hell Knoxie!" He shouts at her. "I said no!"

"And why the fuck not?"

"Because I've already lost too many people I fucking love! If anything, and I mean anything, fucking happened to you, I'd chase down the son of bitch, feed him his balls for brunch and wear his liver like a fucking top hat. I'd write your name in his blood before watching the light fade from his life only to come and take my own knowing I could never fucking live with myself if so much as a goddamn scratch happened that I could've prevented. So just fucking listen to me one goddamn time, at least fucking today, and stay the fuck here." Madden's graphic declaration touches a nerve I didn't think it would.

Huh. Yeah. That's pretty much how I fucking feel at the moment.

Surprisingly enough Knox surrenders in a fluster. "Fuck! Fine! Whatever! Just go! Be safe."

He nods harshly and looks at me. "Move it."

Without real time to think things through, I hurry out the door behind Madden. Wrench's lips move, his voice trying to reach my ears, but the only thing I can focus on is finding Azura before they do.

Even if she hates me or never wants to see me again, I have to at least make sure she's alive. I don't know if I could live with myself if she paid for the error of my ways...if she paid for my stupid fucking mistake. I should've listened to Madden. I should've backed down.

Flying downtown at speeds that would concern most people, I try to bat down as much anxiety as I can needing the clearest head possible. The second I park, I stumble off my bike and scramble to get inside of Mickey's.

155

Relieved at the immediate sight of her pouring a beer for Spencer, I try to ignore the idea that she ran straight to him for comfort.

Now's not the best time for a jealous spat. Remind me of that in a sec.

I approach the bar quickly. "Thank God you're safe."

Unimpressed by my presence she drops her hands on the counter. "I'm not really in the mood McCoy."

Fighting the urge to be hurt by the comment, my mouth drops open to explain just as the beer bottle Spencer is holding shatters, the humming of a bullet passing by reverberating throughout the room. Alarm instantly fills the bar in the form of shrieks and bodies determined to find safe keeping. Another bullet blazes by before I have the chance to dodge out of the way. Instead of piercing me, Spencer cries out in pain, falling off his stool.

"Get down!" I shout to Azura, dropping lower, another shot fired.

On instinct, I stay low to the ground dodging around bigger targets of tables and chairs, in hopes if they do aim for me, that's what will be hit instead. Azura crawls to the corner of the bar, fear dripping from her big brown eyes.

Grateful she's safe, but knowing we need to move, I command, "Do everything I say."

Rapidly her head nods. "Yeah."

The sound of bullets lightens up for a split moment before it seems to increase in volume. Recognizing the sound of more guns being fired at the same time, I lead us even lower to the ground towards the direction of the kitchen. A bottle crashes in front of Azura and she shrieks terrified. My heart aches. I grit my teeth to propel past the agony. Still out of sight we manage to make it through the kitchen door. Finally able to scurry to our feet, I grab her hand and pull her around the cooking station, the shouting from the cook so weak it barely registers. Outside I press us against the wall, put a finger to my lips, and slowly advance us towards the corner. When we arrive, I peer around to see three shooters, helmets still covering their faces, stalking back and forth in front of Mickeys.

"Damn it," I whisper, my motorcycle right in the hot zone.

Knowing the only choice we have is to wait until they venture inside to go after Azura, I stare on, breath choked out of me. As predicted, they enter the wreckage, people fleeing from the bar.

At that moment I tug her hand for us to rush for my bike. Swiftly, we both get our helmets on and bike started before the shooters take notice.

"Hold on!" I shout only seconds before bullets whiz by us.

We peel off down the road, trouble not far behind us. Weaving us around traffic, thankful it's light, I take a sharp left with the intention to head for the highway. Azura's grip around my waist stiffens severely. The feeling of her body trembling for the wrong reasons causes me to accelerate in determination to get her somewhere she's protected.

"Call Big D," I announce into my helmet.

Bluetooth helmets are amazing for the record.

It only rings once before his voice floods my ears. "You got her?"

"Yeah-"

"Thank fuck," Drew sighs in the phone. "Madden's got Angela. He's relocating her to some friends close to the state line."

"Good," my voice barely gets out before the three attackers fly on the highway behind me. "I've got a problem."

"Company?"

"Times three." Weaving around a soccer mom clearly in the wrong lane, I question, "You remember how to get on?"

"Yeah. Yeah. Yeah," Drew grumbles. "Give me a sec."

"I don't really have a sec," I mumble back.

After a short pause Drew shouts, "Goddamn it, Destin! This is a lotta fucking porn bro. Even for you."

"Focus."

"Focus on deleting your browsing history," he gripes. Annoyed I prepare to snap when he announces, "I've got you on the grid. I see the bogie's approaching. Damn. They're tight."

"Tell me about it," I cut off a corvette who doesn't take it well.

They never do.

"Get me somewhere safe," my demand is followed by the tinking sound of a bullet hitting the corvette.

They're not gonna take that well either.

"Next exit," Drew states. "Then cut all the way to the first parking lot you see."

Checking my mirror at the shooters after us, I let out a deep breath and wait to cut between the two cars until the last possible moment, nearly getting my back tire tapped. Off the exit, I dart to the furthest possible lane, swing into the parking lot, and try to be thankful that now there's only two drivers on my ass.

"Follow it around back. You're gonna see a walking path. Take it."

I weave around the speed bumps, Azura's nails cutting into my flesh, reminding me exactly why I can't hesitate or question Drew's instructions.

For the record, I prefer to be the one behind the keyboard.

On a harsh jerk we hop the curb and dash down the vacant trail.

"Listen closely," he says very slowly. "There's gonna be a bridge. Don't take it. Skid across the creek on the left side four feet. Exactly four feet, Triple D."

"I don't exactly have a fucking a ruler, Big D!"

He chuckles. "Trust me."

With the area he is describing on the horizon, the realization of where we are causes me to smirk. "You son of a bitch..."

Thrusting us forward for the creek, I hit the targeted area, while one of the driver's tries to roll up beside me a few inches over jamming his bike directly into a rock that sends him and his motorcycle packing.

"Middle Man scared me shitless that day."

"Yeah," Drew chuckles. "You were such a pussy."

"Fuck you."

Mom loved to find little less known parks and creeks to let us go crazy at, especially in the summer time. This is the one where Daniel hid under the water by that stupid fucking rock while Drew and Madden convinced me to go check it out, so he could scare the shit out of me. Which he did. Assholes...Don't laugh!

Veering back onto the path, Drew states, "Just one left?"

"Right."

There's a faint sound of typing as we pull into a neighborhood. The bike begins to gain on me, fear rising once more that I might be out of time.

Abruptly Drew yells, "Left!"

I take a sharp turn, Azura's sharp gasp the reminder I needed that I can't let fear get the better of me. To my surprise the bike follows with little hesitation on a turn most people would fall off.

"Right!" I take another one with the same unexpected zest hoping to throw him off his game. "Left. Left. Loopy Loo."

No he's not having a fucking stroke.

His directions land us on a road filled with parked cars as expected. Spotting the target in sight, I hop onto the sidewalk for a few houses before crossing the street right in front of the shooter to head back the direction we just came. He follows in the street turning his bike around gracefully. Accelerating I hop back onto the sidewalk opposite of the one I was just on, repeating the previous action once more cutting him off abruptly to travel on the other side. Again he avoids crashing into me while driving parallel onto the street. When I hit the same distance as before, I veer in front of him, and back onto the other sidewalk. This time when I prepare to cross the street, he hops in front of me to beat me to the sidewalk, anticipating me to unexpectedly stop, which is when I stay on the street as he crashes into the fire hydrant he wasn't aware was on the other side of the parked car.

Without waiting to see if he survived, I zoom down the street. "Where am I headed, Big D?"

He feeds me the next line of directions and instantly I know exactly where he's sending us.

I know I asked for safe, but fuck me....it's the last place I expected to be going.

Azura

Unable to stop shaking, I try to find solace in Destin's arm that's draped around me. The throbbing in my head matches the one in my chest. Tears continue streaming down my face as I gasp for breath after breath.

The door finally opens and an older toffee colored man with a beard darts his eyebrows down. "A McCoy on my doorstep is never a good thing."

Destin slightly shrugs. "Sorry Commissioner. But um....it's an emergency."

"It always is with your family," he sighs. "Get in."

"Thank you," Destin softly says leading us past him.

Through blurry eyes, I follow the Commissioner around past a set of stairs and into a living room, the entire time with Destin's arm trying to keep me from collapsing.

Can you blame me? I was just shot at! At least I think it was me they were shooting at. But why on earth would anyone be shooting at me!?

When we drop down on the couch, he sits across from us in a large chair. The expression on his face puts the word displeased to shame. "Why are you here, Destin?"

He hesitates but then questions, "How'd you know it was me?"

"I've spent enough time with Drew to know the difference. You bastards may be identical to the rest of the world, but you have enough characteristics that separate you naturally. As in when you're not trying to be the same person, at the same time....now I will not repeat the question."

Destin sighs, "I need to know why Azura was in the WITSEC program."

"What?" I snap pushing myself out his grip. "I'm not in the WITSEC program!"

The Commissioner ignores my outbreak. "What do you mean *was*?"

Leaning back he struggles to say, but eventually reveals, "The information was leaked. The BV MC is who is after her. Now we both know I could log onto a computer and find out everything you law enforcement poorly hide, but obviously I need more than just that information. I need help. Real help. Please."

He grumbles under his voice before a woman enters the room. "Make the call, Nick." When his eyes dart up to her she firmly points. "Make. The. Call."

With a surrendering of his hands, he stands up. "Give me a few. And don't even think about putting your feet on my coffee table."

Destin nods and before I can ask any more questions, the sweet woman, comes closer. "Nice to finally meet you, Destin. I'm Nadie."

He shakes her hand. "Nice to meet you too."

She extends her hand for me. "Hi honey. What's your name?"

Through sniffles I try to gain some composure. "Azura."

A soft smile comes to her face. "You two look like you could use a little homemade comfort. How about I whip some up? Have you two eaten?"

After glancing at me Destin replies, "I had a bagel."

Recalling the breakfast I dropped all over the floor in shock from catching my supposed boyfriend with my stepsister, I shake my head. "I uh...I haven't eaten."

"Can't have that," Nadie says sweetly. "Let me slip in the kitchen and see what I can cook up."

Almost as soon as she disappears, I snap my head at Destin. "How did you know I was in WITSEC? Am in it? Was? Whatever!"

"I-"

"And how did you know they were coming for me? How do you know who they are?"

"I-"

"Are you one of them?" I scoot my body towards the other end of the couch. "Why do I feel like I don't even know you? One minute you're just the hot guy I've been dreaming of for the past couple years and the next you're trying to bang my sister hours before you're getting me shot at! What the hell is going on?"

Destin lets out a deep breath. "First and foremost, nothing happened with your sister-"

"Sure."

"Nothing. Fucking. Happened." He accents each word so harshly it hurts. "If I wanted to fuck Angela I would've way back when Daniel was passing her around. The only person I've ever wanted to be with, and I mean really be with, is you."

I sniffle away the last of my tears. "How'd you know about WITSEC? I don't even know about it..."

A dismal expression plants itself on his face. "You know how I work another job?"

Trying to lighten the situation I ask, "Are you a secret spy?"

His appreciation of the joke is apparent by the way the corners of his lips twitch. In a hushed tone he answers, "For the last few years my brothers and I have been working for essentially...a drug lord."

This information doesn't blow me out of the water like it probably would most.

Come on now. I'm not a complete idiot. Most of the people I hang around are involved in something illegal. Jamie's fights aren't

168

exactly legal. I've catered to enough underground street racers at the bar to know they're a very real thing. Even the extreme sports I film are not exactly on the right side of the law.

After looking behind me for sight of the Commissioner I question, "Doing what?"

"Our hands have always been typically clean. More delivery of...things," he explains staying vague. "When we were younger it felt like it was worth it. Endless cash. Endless women. Endless security, but then things went sour and he's made it his mission to kill everyone we love-"

"Love?" I interrupt again. "Are you saying-"

"Yeah." Destin moves his body towards me. "That's exactly what I'm saying."

My mouth slips open, but instead of saying it back, I lunge forward and lock our lips. He takes the impact poorly, tumbling backwards, but threads his fingers through my hair to keep the kiss going. Our tongues connect expressing everything the two of us have been failing to say. The kiss is shorter lived than I want, but I know we need to keep talking.

His mouth slips off of mine as he rests his forehead against mine. With his eyes still closed he whispers, "Hi..."

Expanding my smile, I nuzzle his nose until he opens his eyes to see me. "Hi..."

"Are you seriously making out on my couch?" The Commissioner growls entering the room.

Instantly we sit back up and my face blushes. "I'm...I'm sorry. It wasn't what it looked like."

"For everyone in this room's sake it damn sure better not have been what it looked like," he comments flopping down in the chair with his phone in his hand. "Here's the deal. I'm gonna read you why she was in WITSEC then you're gonna tell me why she's no longer in it. Agreed?"

"Agreed," Destin whispers.

The Commissioner touches his phone. "Azura Rose became the name of a four year old born Michelle Kelly." There's a pause in his voice as it seems he's scanning the information. "Her and her mother entered the program as volunteers, which was recommended. It says there was another family entering the program at the same time as you in which your mother had a faint connection with."

"My step dad?"

"Says here, him and his daughter of the same age were entering the program after a recommendation as well. His wife did classified work for the military," he continues to read. "Most of this is blacked out...um...says it was suggested they pretend to be a married couple. His wife and your father knew each other in boot camp. Says your father died while deployed."

In disbelief over the information being shoved at me, I shake my head. "I...I don't remember anything about him. How old was I when he died?"

There's a short hum from him. "Says you were just six months old."

Is that why my mother's so distant from me? Do I look too much like my father? Does it hurt for her to see the life she left behind? I mean, I get now why we don't have photos, but did the fear of the past catching up force her to turn away from me?

"Why are they in the program?" Destin prods. "What did she do?"

"It's what she *saw*," he corrects. "It's listed you witnessed a member of BV MC commit a crime." When he looks up he sighs, "Typically we don't put four years old on the stand, but back when this happened they were desperate to get members of BV MC anyway they could on any charge they could. It was back when the club was setting fires just to watch everything burn."

"Are we talking actual fires or metaphorical ones?" My boyfriend asks.

Fair question.

"Both." The Commissioner clears his throat. "From what I know about them, they went to war hard in the beginning with rival gangs, but over the last few years have dialed it back. More importantly, I don't want them in my city. I have enough shit to deal with between street races, underground fights, drugs and now high price escorts on top of the *normal* crime in a city. I'm aiming to make it less corrupt, not bring in another reason for my beard to go gray. Your turn McCoy. Explain."

Destin's thumbs twiddle. "You um...you know the anonymous reports you've been receiving in regards to The Devil?"

Metaphorical right? He's not trying to tell me that he's seen the actual red faced, pointed horned thing. What do you mean that's

172

not what he looks like? You really wanna have that conversation right now?

"You mean the ones that have helped us cease millions of dollars in assets? Prevent him from fleeing the country? Clear out warehouses and stop a few transports in progress?"

"Those would be them." When The Commissioner glares, Destin finishes, "Apparently he doesn't appreciate it...so he retaliated by leaking Azura's information to the BV MC."

"Just hers," The Commissioner informs. "No one else in her family has had their information revealed. From what the tech team briefly gathered, Azura Rose has been exposed, but the rest of her family seems legit still. Looks more like this nice family adopted you than two families protected under one law."

"I really don't know what the report is talking about," I interject. "Honestly, I don't remember anything before life with Angela and Mark. My mom never talks about it, which makes sense now why, but that part of my memory is non-existent. So even if you could charge them with something I would be useless. Why come after me?"

"Loose ends," Commissioner Carter answers shortly. "Smart criminals typically don't like them."

173

Destin glances away but doesn't comment.

"You said you wanted my help," he grabs his attention again. "What do you want from me?"

"I want help keeping Azura and her family safe."

"Her parents are still out of the country, so they *are* safe. I informed someone to make a call advising they stay that way. I would recommend her sister relocates for a few days while I see if there's anything I can do to help get this settled before my streets become a war zone." He briefly pauses. "A bigger war zone."

"What about me?" my voice meekly questions.

"You have two choices," the Commissioner starts. "I can call the Marshals. We can get you relocated. New identity. It'll be abrupt, take a couple hours, but it can be done. You will no longer exist. We kill Azura Rose and you will become someone else entirely. No contact with any of your friends. Your family. No one. You may have no remaining ties to the person you are now."

Tears sting the corner of my eyes as I glance at Destin who looks like he's about to break down as well. With a trembling jaw I try to ask what the alternative is, but can't seem to get my vocal chords in gear.

Destin fingers intertwine with mine, planting a kiss on the back of it. Turning to face The Commissioner he asks, "What's the other choice?"

He folds his hands together. With his eyes placed on me he states, "You can let the McCoys protect you." Surprised by his words my eyebrows lift. "If there's anything I've learned over the past few months, it's the lengths they are willing to go to protect the ones they love. In my opinion, you're safer and most likely happier with them watching over you. Merrick brought my daughter home from the pits of hell. I have no doubt Destin will die trying to make sure you don't fall into the flames. However, the choice is ultimately yours. Regardless of your choice, I will be working to keep the BV MC out of my city."

Destin turns to look at me. "It's up to you baby. If I've gotta live the rest of my life without you so you're safe I will." My breath feels robbed from me. "But if you choose to stay, you heard what he said. I'll die trying to save you if necessary."

"My whole life is here," I whisper softly. "I mean, I know it's not big, and I know nothing really feels like home, but there are things I don't wanna give up. Especially you."

175

His tongue wets his lips fighting the instinct to kiss me.

Probably best with the Police Commissioner watching.

"I'll do what I can from my end. I'll have an unmarked officer on detail duty as often as I can spare the man power. Most likely round the clock."

"Thank you." Wiping away the tears from the corner of my eyes, I nod again. "Thank you so much."

The Commissioner nods in return before moving his attention to Destin. "McCoy."

"Yeah?"

"I've told you and your brothers, but since you all seem to have a comprehension issue I will repeat myself one more time. Back. The. Hell. Off." Destin's grip tightens. "I know how badly you want The Devil. All of you. However, at this point, I need you and your brothers to back down. Yes, the tips were appreciated, but it's not worth the price of the bodies that keep falling on my conscience."

Wait. Is that why Daniel died? Merrick? No one has mentioned the details. The only thing they say is there was an incident....what else am I missing? Do you know?

"We can handle him if you'll just take a step back. I need you to trust me. I have an inside man. The walls are closing in around The Devil. He's scared. He's moving right where I need him too, so one final time. Back. Off." When Destin looks like he's about to object The Commissioner adds, "If not for my sake then for hers. You've seen what he's capable of."

Do you have any idea what that is? I mean can it get any worse than letting the entire world know I'm wanted by a motorcycle gang? Why are you looking at me like that?

After a meal of bacon mac and cheese filled with lighter conversation from Nadie while The Commissioner disappeared to find ways to help, Destin drives us back to the apartment. We lounge around in the living room watching movies in an active attempt to keep our minds busy as we wait for Madden's return. Once he's back, he assures us Angela is safe, and that the best thing we can do right now is try to get some rest.

Destin takes his advice and leads us into his bedroom.

The door shuts behind me. Almost immediately I say, "Wait. I...I don't....I don't have anything here."

Destin lifts his eyebrows in confusion. "What?"

"Clothes," I start. "Or deodorant. Or a tooth bush. I don't have anything here, Destin. My stuff-"

"We can swing by your place tomorrow and grab some," he says pulling me into him by the hand. "We'll go with Madden. We'll pack you up and move you here until...until..."

"Until when?" my voice chokes out. "What if The Commissioner can't help? What if I'm never safe again? What if-"

"As long as you're with me, you'll always be safe." Destin pushes a fallen strand behind my ear. "I promise."

Nodding, I let out a breath I didn't realize I had been holding.

Playfully he says, "You can't use my toothbrush, because I think that's gross to share, but I can offer you a t-shirt to sleep in."

A small smile flashes on my face.

He strolls away, grabs me a plain black t-shirt, and proceeds to strip out of the clothes from the day. As soon as we're both dressed for bed, we crawl under the sheets, and let the mindless ramble of an old re-run of a sitcom attempt to entertain us.

Is it weird that this feels perfect? I've spent my entire life wanting somewhere that feels like people can see me, like I matter and here I am, getting exactly what I used to lie in bed and wish for. Is it the ideal situation? Absolutely fucking not. Is this family or my boyfriend perfect? No. But at least I feel like I belong. At least I feel like if I went missing or into hiding, he would notice. He would care. None of my family has made contact. Not even my parents.

Eventually the weight of my thoughts rolls me over onto my side. Admiring Destin's profile, I lightly run my finger along his jawbone line. His eyes briefly shut in what appears to be a pleasant way. They flicker open again until my finger repeats the action.

Quietly he sighs, "That feels amazing."

"I'm barely touching you."

"Yeah," Destin hums. "But *you're* barely touching me. Every little thing about you feels like the best thing to ever happen to me." He turns to face me. "Everything. I'm the luckiest man in the entire fucking world and I don't deserve to be."

179

My finger strokes the spot once more and he melts into it. "Would you really have been okay letting me go?"

"No fucking way," he grunts. "Losing you would be the final blow of lost family I could possibly take. I'd fucking stop waiting for whatever plan it is Madden thinks he has building, locate The Devil, and place a bullet between eyes."

The violent declaration should scare me, should freak me out, but it does just the opposite. I find extreme comfort in it.

Is that twisted? You know...I don't even care if it is.

"I'd let you go because your life is a million times more important than mine."

"Not true," I quietly object. With the tip of my finger, I turn his head so our eyes can meet. "You undersell yourself too often. If you're the luckiest man, it's only because I'm the luckiest woman. I love you, Destin McCoy, and that's something I couldn't live with walking away from."

Slowly his mouth descends to mine. Instantly swept away in the magic that comes every time our lips connect, I run my hand around to his nape where I hold on for dear life. There's a mixture of a moan and sob that come from him as he grips my hip with the same amount of gusto. In a gentle yet intense session of kisses the one article of clothing each of us is wearing disappears. Our bodies fervently grind against one another, legs rubbing together as if they've began the sexual journey without us. More belated than either of us clearly enjoys by the eager clawing we've begun, Destin's cock nudges inside my tense muscles. A long relieved moan seeps from me as the leg that's dangling over his hip is moved putting his shaft at a deeper angle when he shifts to palm my ass.

With his face buried in my neck, I softly proclaim, "*This* feels amazing."

Like the most heavenly treat he's ever tasted, he continues indulging, each suck in unison with his thrusts. The sharp pushes of his dick not only penetrate deep but tease my clit with ephemeral grazes. Craving more, I arch into him. My arm that's draped around him finally moves to anchor myself for the imminent orgasm that's impatiently waiting.

"Just a little more," I beg.

He squeezes my ass tighter. A loud moan escapes, which is when Destin's tongue drags itself up to my ear. "You can have anything you want from me, baby. Just ask."

I whimper at his words as does my pussy. The muscles are wound so tightly around his cock, I'm afraid if he tries to change angles, it'll snap it in half as punishment.

I don't know that you can actually break a dick in half, but you can injure one! Had a guy at the bar tell me that horror story.

The smooth ball of his ring rolls around my earlobe. "Tell me what you want, Azura."

I bite down on my bottom lip holding back screams. Not pleased with the choice, his teeth clamp down.

On a sharp shriek I demand, "To come! Destin make me come!"

And with those words he fiercely drills into me. His hips jerk repeatedly, so relentless I'm not sure my pussy will survive what it's asking for. Suddenly the mixture of clit teasing and g-spot nudging causes me to shut my eyes tightly before his name pours out of me. My pussy throbs and throbs begging helplessly as I spiral out of control, careless about who hears. The intense squeezes are rewarded with a hot stream that feels as if it's endless. Faintly, he calls my name in my ear, the sound of it more like an invocation than I've ever heard before. Completely exhausted, emotionally and physically, the two of us crumple together in a sweltering pile of limbs.

I'm glad I chose to stay. I'd rather live happily for a few more days than return to a version of the miserable existence being with him has allowed me to give up.

Destin

What if Azura staying was a terrible idea? I mean I love her. I know we can keep her safe, but what if this shit is much worse than I thought? What if that unmarked car across the street isn't enough when the shit really gets thick? What if The Devil has an inside man the way The Commissioner does. To be fair he used to have a shit ton, but they started to drop like flies a couple months ago. What if no matter what we do it's never enough? What if the only way the BV MC gives up is if she really is dead? Should we fake her death? Why aren't you giving me any answers?

"Destin!" Drew's voice snaps.

Unsure of why he's yelling I turn abruptly and bite back. "What?"

"Can you hand me that wrench or not?"

"Yeah." I shake away the invading thoughts. Reaching for it, I ask, "Why'd you yell at me?"

"Because I've asked you for that so many times, Wrench is probably beginning to think I'm in love with him."

"I was flattered," Wrench calls from across the shop.

A light chuckle leaves Drew as he takes the tool. "Look, I know you're worried-"

"I'm fine."

"You're not," my brother shuts me down. "It's only been a few days. We all know this kinda shit takes some time. Try to relax. We won't let anything happen to her."

I can't relax. The only thing that remotely gets my mind off of possibly losing her is fucking her and I can't fuck her when I'm supposed to be in the shop. Well, I mean I can, but they only let me get away with that shit the first two days. Since I've been back down here I've tried to spend most of my time behind the computer, catching up on paperwork and fucking The Devil over in every little hole I can. Yeah, I know what The Commissioner said, but come on. I'm a McCoy. How well do you think we listen to what the cops say?

"Did you hear a word I just said?" Drew gripes. When my head tilts to answer he surrenders his hands. "Never mind. Just do me a favor?"

"What's that?"

He drops an arm around my shoulder and turns us to face a Harley pulling into the driveway of the shop. "Look at that. I mean just look at that Triple D. Don't you wanna run your fingers down those sexy curves, grip that bitch, and show her the best fucking time possible." With a small smile I nod in agreement. "Ride that from sunrise to sunset. Damn. Go talk to her and convince her to leave that precious piece of ass here for us to touch." He points at me. "Don't blow it. I haven't touched a Harley that sexy in a while."

Rolling my eyes I grab my tablet and hustle out of the shop towards the leather clad woman who is still straddling her bike.

Professionally, I introduce myself. "I'm Destin McCoy. How may I help you?"

In a swift motion she moves her helmet, ruffles her red hair, but doesn't remove her sunglasses. "Just the man I wanted to see."

Alarm alerts my system into action. Holding the tablet with one hand, I drop the other, preparing to give the hand signal for back up.

Yeah. We've got fucking hand signals. When you switch from heavily guarded to heavily, violently pursued, you invest in that kind of simple shit.

"Relax," she says leaning forward. "I'm gonna talk. You're gonna listen. Every word I say will appear to be said in a threatening form. That's the intent. Play along. Got it?"

"Who the hell are you?"

"I'm undercover agent Clara Louis. I received a message if I had any information that could help to make contact." She messes with her red hair once more. "This conversation never took place."

Relieved that my luck might be changing, I nod. "Never."

"Good." After a glance over my shoulder she cocks her head at me. "Years ago when BV MC was trying to make giant waves among their rivals, particularly the ZD MC, there was an incident and an object of their victory was acquired. This was a huge deal. The reasons exactly are legends that change depending who tells the story. However, this object, went missing a few years back after a party."

"What is the object?"

"The only information I have on that is it has something to do with a scorpion."

"And Azura?"

"The incident occurred at the ZD President's house while his wife and child weren't home. Apparently Azura used to live in the same neighborhood, was outside playing, and was the only one who spotted him fleeing with the object. The BV member was Slaughter. He's now President. If she can place his face at that scene, he faces the possibility of prison because the ZD president was also murdered that day, around that time. Any guesses who they wanna pin for it?"

The information has me uncomfortably shifting my weight. "But she doesn't remember anything."

Clara shrugs. "That's good. Add that with the little peace offering of the missing object and they would back off. Hell, they'd probably do more than that. Might give a chance to be a prospect."

Never happening.

"At this point, it's just her word of lack of memory versus Slaughter's determination to keep his presidency. Look, he's an irrational man, one of the worst actually, but he's a man with a strict honor code. Give him your word and bare a gift he wants, free passage from whatever it is you want. *Including* your girlfriend's life spared. He takes loyalty pledges, oaths, and protecting his family to the grave."

"If you know he's committed murder-"

"Allegedly," she corrects. "The evidence of that entire situation is a mess. Honestly, it's been too long for her witness testimony to mean shit, putting aside the fact she was just a child, but he doesn't realize that or it's not setting in." Clara prepares to put her helmet back on. "Find whatever it is they want and make peace. Make a bond. You should know the first time they sent prospects to kill her. The next time it won't be amateurs."

Those were fucking amateurs?

"You haven't got long before Slaughter is going to want to act again. He's got more pressing business on the docket, but not for much longer, so act fast." I attempt to say something when she cuts me off, "I have to go. Anyone asks what happened here and I threatened to make you choke on your balls if you didn't produce the girl soon."

With a new task tumbling around in my head, I compliment. "Nice bike by the way."

Clara winks. "Perk when you're fucking the VP."

189

After she gives me a good rev, she backs her bike up slowly, the unmarked cop stationed across the street now on edge. I turn quickly to head back into the shop.

"I told you *not* to scare her off," Drew jokes until he sees the expression on my face. "Wait. What the fuck just happened?"

"Um..."

"Who was that?"

"BV MC," I smoothly lie.

"Are you fucking kidding?" He tenses. "Why didn't you say something fucking sooner?"

"She just...came to send a message."

"What was it?"

Staring into the eyes of one of the only people I've never lied to, I swallow the knot of guilt.

We have to keep this a secret. At least until I can figure out what it is that went missing. Once I've got that information, I'll share. I'll bring it to Madden's attention too. It'll be my saving grace for fucking not listening when he demanded it before. As for now, this is just between us. Got it?

"Just..."

Drew folds his arms across his chest. "Just what?"

"Just...just that we don't have much time to give them Azura."

Sensing the lie he scrunches his face tightly. "Is that all?"

Instead of risking my voice shaking, the indication of a lie, I nod. Drew stares harshly, the cycle of disappointment and betrayal clear as the sky outside.

He sighs, "I guess I'll give Mad Man a call to let him know." When I don't object he storms away kicking a tool out of the way, which catches Wrenches attention.

Triple D doesn't lie to each other. It was a promise we lived by when we were growing up. We would lie to other people. Lie about each other if it could help any other brother get laid, but we swore we'd always be honest to each other. But what do you want from me? Desperate times and all that bullshit. It's just not Triple D I'm trying to protect any more. It's the love of my life too.

191

Destin

Azura's voice invades the bathroom just seconds after the warm water falls down my back. "I'm serious Destin."

Annoyed this argument is still in motion I roll my eyes. "Azura-"

"No." she stubbornly cuts me off. "I have given up staying at my house. I can't go back to the bar not only because it's still closed, but because they might try to get me there too. I *need* this Destin. I need to do this event tomorrow. If it'll make you feel better to be at my side with your superman cape then by all means join me, but I'm going."

My face appears around the shower curtain. Seeing the stern but sad expression, I cave. "Fine. I'll go too. Get up ass early and everything for you. Now, get naked so I can fuck you rotten before I have to get to work. It's all hands on deck today."

She grins widely, my favorite color coating her cheeks. Slowly Azura pulls my t-shirt over her head, the sight underneath stiffening my shaft.

We grabbed her shit from her house over a week ago and still she prefers sleeping in my shirts. It's probably the sexiest look of all time. Find me a dude who argues that point and I'll be the first one to label him full of shit.

Azura slinks her body over to me, dangling the temptation she is at a frustrating distance. As soon as she's within reach, I yank her to the edge of the shower, and roughly suck her nipples into my mouth. Her moans, which are music to my ears, echo in the shower. After lapping at each of the sensitive peaks, she slips into the shower. Unable to control myself I drop my face to her pussy where I spread her thighs and bury my tongue. The first lick elicits a loud enough cry that encourages me to continue. Ruthlessly I feast, each flavor filled suck doing it's best to soothe the desperate sexual deviant inside that always feels insatiable. My tongue twirls around her clit, toying with it until she's falling apart. Committed to the notion of turning her pussy into the trembling tender tranquility my cock can't wait to further please, I continue my movements until she erupts all over my tongue. Rising to my feet, I turn her around. She braces her hands on the tile wall. With her legs spread she sticks her ass slightly out allowing me to push my cock home. We groan in unison. My hands clutch her hips as I bounce her beautifully on my dick. Each precise push receives an echoed praise creating the most remarkable erotic symphony. Lost in the nirvana that can only be felt when I'm with her, I continue to pump, my cock knocking at her g-spot so feverishly she comes again within the first few minutes.

Feeling gluttonous, I don't slow down knowing the only thing I want on her mind while I'm away is me.

Azura cries out, her hand hitting the wall. "I can't take anymore."

"Just a little more baby," my encouragement is proceeded with me giving her ass a good pop. The smacking sound swells my dick in warning I don't have long left. I repeat the action. "Take that dick just a little longer." She moans hungrily at the following pops. I growl harshly each time. One last blow is delivered before her pussy clasps onto my cock so brutally, it caves, coming faster than I can possibly stop it. "Fuck...."

"My God," her voice agrees.

In one easy movement, I cradle her body to mine, littering her neck with kisses. When my lips roll around to her ear, I whisper, "I love you..."

"I love you too."

Hearing the proclamation eases the worry I can't seem to stop from falling into. Between continuing to close The Devil's operations at every opportunity that presents itself and sleepless nights researching the object the BV MC is missing, I've began to

wonder how much longer I can keep the inevitable implosion at bay.
Are you getting the feeling it's not too much longer?

Azura

You know you don't really know how much you miss gallivanting around the outside world until it's taken away as an option. Sure being stuck in the apartment has some perks. Lots of sex. I mean lots of sex. After Destin and I are done most of the time it takes me at least an hour to remember how to walk again. Plus, I get to work on this little gift I've been putting together for him, which is going to be epic. However, I do miss seeing my friends. The bar. Jamie has swung by for a brief visit, but Spencer who took a pretty brutal shot has barely made contact. I got a message saying he needed some space for healing, but that was on my old phone that I haven't used in the last week. I've given him my new number. But still nothing...

Angela called to apologize profusely to me and Destin about the incident. She spent the entire time talking about how she wasn't in a good place, how much she misses Daniel, and how thankful she is the McCoy's rescued her yet again. Not once does she ask or allow me to fill her in on my own safety. My parents aren't much better. They called to double check that Angela was somewhere safe and that I wasn't going to stay at the house, but that was it. Part of me feels like they all wish I would just die or at least go back into WITSEC without them. I highly doubt they'd blink an eye if I did.

Melody, Drew's girlfriend twirls around in the kitchen, twisting her hips to music while she adds cheese to the salad.

Not only is this woman breathtakingly beautiful, Drew worships the ground she walks on. She sat down one afternoon while the guys were at work and told me how they got together. Turns out it's a doozy. Just one you have to hear for yourself. The other upside of her is that she's stuck in this apartment worse than I am. I can visit the outside world when Destin's in a giving mood. She can't. Not yet. Not while the man known as The Devil is still alive. Sometimes I think late at night Drew sneaks her out, but don't tell anyone. I don't want anyone in trouble.

My cell phone buzzes across the bar, pausing my work on the computer. The number makes me grin. "Hey Spencer!"

"Az," his voice softly greets in return. "You doin' okay?"

"Yeah." I lean back in the bar chair. "I mean as fine as a person can be after everything that happened. What about you? Are you okay? How's the injury?"

"I'll be fine," he replies. "Still a bit painful, but nothing major got hit. Well other than my pride."

Confused, I ask, "Why your pride?"

197

"Because I should've been the one to save you," his sigh hurts my heart. "Because even wounded I should've at least been smart enough to tell you to get down. To come after you....anything. Something."

"You did what anyone would do if they were being shot at, Spence." Melody stops her sultry dancing to give me a suspicious look. I mouth the word. "Friend." She nods her approval and returns to moving in ways that make me believe Drew is probably a lucky guy.

Really lucky if she rocks like that in the bedroom. Oh what! Come on! You were thinkin' it too.

"Really? Is that why Destin knew to at least tell you to get the hell out of the way?" He grumps. "I shouldn't be pissed at the guy for being able to use his brain or saving my best friend..."

I hum my approval of Destin's name.

"Everything okay between you two? He taking good care of you while you're not on bar duty?"

"Yeah. He's great. We're great. I appreciate you asking."

"Did you see that there was only one other person injured?" Spencer's voice cracks.

"I did." Remembering the headline on the front of the paper, thankful my name had not been included at all, I add, "The other person took a leg shot. The entire thing has Mickey in high debates about ever reopening."

"Can't blame him. With rumors swirling his gambling debt is what got his bar shot up in the first place, I would say his smartest move is probably to keep those doors closed."

Mickey's gambling problem is one of those things I'm not sure actually exists. While I'm thankful there's no word out about the BV MC demanding my blood there's too much guilt that comes with someone else's name being tarnished to save mine.

There's a beep on my phone and it's a number I don't recognize. "Hey Spencer, I gotta answer the call on the other line, but promise me I'll see you soon."

"Definitely."

"Take care," I coo before switching to the other line. "Hello."

A man's voice strongly says, "Hello. This is Marshal Mayweather with X-treme X-press. I'm looking for a Miss Azura Rose."

Concerned, I glance at Mel who keeps watching me out of the corner of her eye.

We've become great friends in these past couple of weeks. She knows at the first sign of trouble to flag a McCoy just as well as I do.

Determined to keep my voice from shaking, I steady it. "Um...this is she."

"Good evening Miss Rose. As you recall we interviewed you a few days ago."

They did. It was actually the perk of that day. I kept it to myself though. Figured there was no need to build false hope since there was a good chance I wasn't going to get the job. There were a shit ton of other candidates all probably more qualified than me. I was just thankful they even considered me worth interviewing.

Sorry for calling so late. I had a meeting with Guy Klinger-"

The unexpected frisson causes me to blurt, "The snowboarder?"

"Yes. He's actually a good friend of mine," Marshal brags. "If you accept the job offer, I'll be more than happy to introduce the two of you. Be warned he does have a weakness for girls with beautiful smiles."

"I'm sorry, come again?"

"I'm offering you the job to come work for us," he informs.

My jaw drops to the ground, which pauses Mel's actions again. "You're...You're offering me..."

"A job," Marshall slyly finishes the sentence for me. "That is if you are still interested. We loved the video resume that was initially passed to us. Your interview was charismatic. Your enthusiasm for extreme sports is almost as impressive as your passion for your craft. I think your talent needs to be captured, polished, and presented for the entire world to see."

Unsure of what to say, I whisper, "I...I don't know what to say."

"Well hopefully you say yes," he chuckles. "I'll send you over the paperwork with the details, but what you need to know most importantly is you'll be flying out in two weeks."

Surprised at the timing, I question. "Flying out where?"

"To London."

"For how long?"

"Couple months give or take. There's some basic boring training, blah blah blah, then we'll fly out to Colorado for the WG." With my head spinning faster than my mouth moves, I don't even manage to confirm or deny this is what I want. "Make sure when you sign your contract, it's in blue pen. I really hate black ink."

That's...weird.

"Alright, I have to catch a flight. I have a date. We'll be in touch."

The call ends before I have the chance to voice my opinion on anything.

Did that really just happen to me? Was I really just given my dream job?

202

"I know that look," Melody sighs leaning her hands on the counter across from me.

I dart my head up.

"It's the life changing one."

My mouth moves to explain to her what just happened, to scream at how exciting this is, to scream that maybe getting away while the BV MC is hunting me would be perfect, but instead only air comes out.

This is a good thing right? I mean get my dream job and *stay safe? Destin can come and visit me! Maybe he'd wanna come with me...Am I being selfish?*

There's the sound of a key entering a lock, which is when I close my lap top down.

Don't wanna ruin his surprise.

Suddenly McCoy laughter fills the room. The pair of identical faces makes Melody smile as wide as me.

Destin shakes his head. "I can't believe you bet Wrench over the color of Knox's panties."

"I can't believe he took that bet," Drew chuckles closing the door behind him.

"He almost got knocked out," Destin sighs flopping down at the bar beside me.

His brother nods excitedly, arriving next to Mel. "By *Madden*. That's what makes it funny."

"How is that funny?" Melody questions her boyfriend.

"Because Madden's face turns the color of zit that needs to pop, which leads Knoxie to almost, always apply the unneeded pressure," Drew continues to laugh. "This time, she flashed Wrench her underwear."

Destin shakes his head again. "Madden dented a car hood."

Our jaws drop in unison while Drew continues his snickering. "It was a Lexus. He hates Lexus's."

"Not funny Big D. You know how fucking uncomfortable that phone call was? 'Yes sir. Sorry to inform you there was a minor

204

incident in the shop today. It'll be fixed free of charge along with the other services you brought your vehicle in for.' Not my favorite phone call nor my favorite report to make. Your little joke was an expensive one."

Drew shrugs still smirking. "The funniest ones typically are."

"You are so much trouble," Melody scolds at him.

His smile expands. "That's why you love me."

"Is that why?" she playfully counters.

He moves his body to greet her just as Destin moves his to greet me. The feeling of his hand winding through the back of my hair causes my eyes to close. Our lips find their way to each other, the touching of our tongues brief.

When he pulls away he whispers at me, "Hi..."

"Hi..." I coo in return.

"Smells like heaven," Drew compliments as he washes his hands. "Want us to set the table?"

Melody winks at me before nodding at him. "Please."

She mentioned earlier that Drew was well trained. If she cooks, he can set and clear the table. I've seen him do it once or twice before, but I thought it was a fluke. I didn't realize the McCoys had manners.

Destin hops up to help. "It's just us four. After Drew's little panty prank-"

"Haha, panty prank," he proudly echoes.

"Knox made a comment about needing to go see someone who knew all the colors of her underwear *when* she chose to wear them and Madden made a bunch of unnecessary noise before informing us he needed to get his frustrations out."

"Code for fuck someone 'til he forgets how much he cares about Knox," Drew translates.

"Shouldn't they just...tell each other how they feel?" I suggest.

All three of them give me a sarcastic look.

Why are you giving it to me too? It's not that far-fetched of a notion.

"I highly doubt that'll ever happen," Destin mumbles placing the plates down while Drew does the silverware.

"Better chance of having a snowball fight in hell," Drew's joke gets a smile from his brother.

The four of us settle down at the kitchen table where we fill our plates with homemade lasagna, mozzarella salad, spinach salad, and fresh baked, from scratch garlic bread.

Looks beautiful and can cook like a gourmet chef. Have I mentioned I love her too? She also happens to make a mean set of breakfast tacos.

Conversation flows along with the wine. Glass after glass is had by Mel and Drew until they reach the point of apparent intoxication. While I feel a little tipsy, I'm definitely the most sober with Destin not far behind me.

Which is good because I want to have this conversation at least remotely sober.

Mel giggles, leaning into Drew's arms on the couch. "So, what was the big news, Azura?"

"I've got a *head*line," Drew less than subtly jokes.

"You've got news?" Destin's thumb strokes my shoulder. "What is it?"

I hesitate to answer.

Mel pushes, "Come on. Tell us! We're family, right? We celebrate great news together!"

Wouldn't know. This is like the first good news I've had since I got accepted into college. My parents didn't celebrate with me then, so much as ask how much would the first check be.

"Can we celebrate great news together naked?" Drew whines.

"One track mind," she fusses.

"One track path...to the bedroom."

Destin shakes his head and bumps him. "Come on baby. What's the good news? I'm sure we could all use a little."

Smiling softly I reply, "I got offered my dream job today."

In unison they croak, "What?!"

"Yeah. The biggest name in extreme sports wants me to work for them," I gush trying to hold back my excitement.

"That's fucking incredible," Destin exclaims.

"Does that mean we have to stop watching football?" Drew asks. "Or better yet, is there an extreme football league?"

"Isn't that Rugby?" Destin jokes, causing his brother to laugh before they fist bump again.

They do that a lot. Not just fist bump, but laugh at each other's jokes that are only slightly amusing. It's cute and sad.

"If I take the job, I start in two weeks," I continue slowly.

Mel looks puzzled. "If? What do you mean if? Don't you mean when?"

"Yeah," Destin adds. "When, right?"

My eyes fall into his, the debate of correcting them so difficult, dinner starts to churn in my stomach. Finally I confess, "I'd have to relocate to London for a couple months before traveling to Colorado for a week."

"London baby!" Drew shouts. "Remember that episode of Friends?"

Destin's eyes never leave mine. "So...you'd have to leave me?"

"Well-"

"Here."

"I-"

"You're just gonna up and go without thinking about how this could affect us?"

His rush of irritation hits me like shot gun blasts.

"You're just gonna throw away these last few weeks, all we've done to protect you for some...fucking job?"

"Ohhh...." Mel's voice whispers. "Oh no..."

"Bro," Drew tries to help.

"How the hell could you do this to us?" Destin bites. "How the hell could I, could all of us mean so fucking little to you?"

"Excuse me?" I snap.

"Bro," Drew tries to intervene once more.

"I risk my fucking life to save yours, bust my ass night after night to find a way to keep you alive, and now it's 'good fucking luck with your life here'? You're not worth a damn?"

"Enough," Drew states.

"Fuck off," Destin grumbles at his brother rising to his feet.

Drew mimics the action. "No, you fuckin' chill."

"Don't fuckin' tell me what to do!" he snaps viciously. "It's not your fucking girlfriend leaving you like you're nothing!"

Baffled almost as much as heartbroken by the words falling freely from him, I meet eyes with Mel who nods at our own spoken conversation.

"And it's not yours doing that bullshit either," Drew informs him. "She didn't *take* the job yet, remember?" The blow pushes his attention to glance away. "Don't be so fucking selfish."

"Why not?" Destin snaps. "You were."

Drew rescued Melody from the hell she was living in. He risked his life to do it. That's selfish, but isn't that the good kind? The okay kind?

Instead of letting them continue to fight Melody stops them when she stands. "Let's go to bed, Drew. Let them...let them have their moment."

Her hand on his yanks him out of the anger induced coma he had slipped into. He delivers one more hard glare to his brother before looking at me. "Congrats on the job offer, Azura. You deserve it."

"Thanks," I whisper in return.

We wait in silence while the two of them disappear into their room. Once the door shuts, Destin's head snaps back down at me, a combination of fear and sadness floating.

In a hushed tone he asks, "Are you gonna take it?"

Unsure I simply shrug.

I wanted too...I wanted to so bad. That's what I wanted before this moment.

"I don't want you to."

"That's pretty clear," I sigh.

"So don't."

Perplexed at his level of sudden narcissism I gripe, "Really? You want me to give up my dream job, my first chance at a career that doesn't involve me smelling like cheap whiskey and curly fries, without a second thought?"

"Yeah," Destin answers without hesitating.

Could he possibly answer that any faster?

"There shouldn't be a second thought Azura. I love you. You belong here. With me."

"Which is why I didn't say yes," I confess softly. "Because I don't wanna be without you."

"Then say no."

"But I don't wanna be stuck here either, Destin. It's hard enough being trapped in this apartment while waiting for my life to end, but I've been at meaningless dead end jobs since I joined the work world. This is the first real chance I have at following my passion and instead of supporting me or offering for us to make this work, you're looking me in the face and forcing me to choose?"

"Yes."

Seriously? Who answers that fast?

"So that's it?" I stand up. "I have to pick between my dream job and my dream love?"

"Yes."

My hand runs through my hair. "There's no way you're willing to make this work?"

"It can't." He shrugs. "I can't save you from overseas. I can't rescue you from another country. I can't protect you from-"

"Why do you think I'm so goddamn defenseless?" I bark. "Like I'm some pathetic damsel in distress who can't climb out her tower without some big burly man?"

"I'm not burly..."

That's what he took from that? This conversation is crashing faster than I realized.

"Destin. I can take care of myself. I took care of myself for *years* before you showed up."

"Because you had too," he argues. "Now you never do. Now you have me. Now you never have to worry again or be afraid or scared, because you have me. Because I'm here."

Shaking my head slowly I counter, "You think that's why I love you? Because you're some security blanket I can't do without? Is this even about me?" When he swallows, it rains down the truth I can't believe I missed. "It's not...This isn't about me leaving. This isn't about some fucked up hero scenario in your head. You're afraid if I leave I won't come back."

Destin bites his bottom lip.

"You're afraid I'm gonna abandon you."

"Why wouldn't I be afraid of that?" His voice shakes. "That's all that ever fucking happens to me! My mom! My dad! My cousin! My brothers! Everyone I love fucking leaves! The only difference is they didn't choose to and you are!"

Feeling a sob come to my throat, I choke it down. "Just because I'm not at your fingertips doesn't mean I'm abandoning you."

"If you get on that plane, that's exactly what you're doing."

Tears strangle my vocal chords from countering. I surrender my hands. "I'm going to bed."

Destin doesn't attempt to stop me. The moment I round the corner for his bedroom, my eye catch sight of Drew whose head is peered around his bedroom door frame. A simple broken smile is offered to me. I give it back with a shrug of my shoulders.

I don't know what to do. About anything.

Destin

A sharp unexpected pain lands in my gut.

What the fuck was that?

Groaning, I lift my eyelids to see Drew peering down over me, an expression so grim I'm not sure I've ever seen it before.

He didn't used to be such a dick in the morning. No. That was Daniel.

"What the fuck is your problem?"

"What the fuck is yours?" he bites back.

Unsure of exactly what's going on I don't answer.

"I should fucking nail you again," he gripes. "Maybe in the dick since that's what you were being."

The memory of last night tumbles back into my throbbing skull. I glance at the coffee table where the bottle of whiskey I went and bought last night stands empty.

Old habits suck.

"We need to talk," Drew informs flopping down on the couch across from me. "Right here. Right now."

"Can it wait?" I groan. "Kinda hungover."

"Good." He nods. "Maybe you'll associate your destructive behavior with your destructive decisions."

"Having a girlfriend is turning you into Dr. Phil."

"Rather that than a dick with legs."

His comment causes me to shift until I'm sitting up.

"Destin, it is not easy being a McCoy," he starts on a deep sigh. Leaning forward to rest his arms on his legs he continues. "It never has been. When we were really little, we all slept in the same room cause that's what we could afford. When we were a little older we had to learn to make it without parents. By the time puberty fucking hit we were hustling because that's what life demanded for us to do." My mouth twitches at the facts. "We're not weak. We weren't made to be weak. We weren't made for the world to keep us down even though that's all it feels like it wants to do." With a shrug his voice drops. "It fucking sucks to be us. To wake up every morning wondering if today is the day we lose someone else we

218

love. To wake up having to be a fucking soldier in a war with no end. To carry around battle scars and open wounds from a lifetime of fucking choices we were never really given. Do not think for one second I am telling you that I don't know the fucking pain you carry around."

My jaw trembles. "What are you saying?"

"That you have a choice to make Destin. Every day. You can wake up, count how many times the world tries to bury you while you battle it or you can wake up and count how many things are worth fighting for while you keep swinging."

There's an immediate ache in my chest. In a choked voice I shake my head. "I'm so goddamn tired of swinging..."

"We all are," he admits. "But the only time, you ever truly lose is when you give up bro. Every fallen McCoy, never gave up." His words push the tears out of my eyes. "I know you love Azura-"

"So fucking much Big D."

"And that girls loves you too. But you can't trap what you love in some sort of weird cage so that it never leaves you. You really love her? You have to have a little faith. The same faith that Mom had every morning when she worried that there wouldn't be enough food to feed us. The same faith Dad when he tucked us in at night before he left for work that he would make enough to keep the lights on. It's the faith of the McCoy. The faith no matter how shitty something seems there's faith that someway, somehow, everything will be alright."

A sniffle comes from me. "But what if it's not? What if-"

"Don't." He stops me. "Don't waste your blows in this world on what ifs. There are too many more important things that need those swings. Let her take that job. Don't turn the thing worth fighting for into the thing you end up fighting. That'll hurt worse than anything else."

There's a sound of footsteps, which draws our eyes to Mel who has entered the room. She's dressed in a black oversized hoodie, black pants, and black shoes. Her attire is my indication for where they are headed to.

To see The Commissioner for their scheduled meeting.

"You ready?" She sweetly asks my brother.

He smiles at her before looking back at me. "Worth. Fighting. For."

I nod. "Yeah. I get it."

"You don't," he sighs as he stands. "But you will..."

Without another word to me he heads for her. Mel asks, "Can we get breakfast? I'm starving."

"We each had that. It was full of protein, remember?"

The dirty joke is filled with laughter short lived, I assume from a playful punch she delivers to him. As soon as they're gone, I stand up and stretch from the uncomfortable night on the couch.

I could've slept in my bed, but it didn't feel right. Not with the way I treated her. God, I was such an idiot last night.

After doing a sweep of the apartment to see Madden and Knox both didn't make it home last night, I venture toward my bedroom, each step more cautious than the last.

Worst case scenario? She calls me a dick, throws something at me, then we make up and have make up sex. I don't care what happens as long as we make up. And....have make up sex.

I give my door a couple knocks and wait for permission to enter. When there's no response, I knock again. With my hand braced on the door knob I announce, "I'm gonna come in, so we can talk, alright?"

There's no objection from the other side so I invite myself in. The vacant room parts my lips.

I lied. This *is the worst possible scenario.*

My eyes search the room in disbelief before darting back to the living room for my cell phone. I grab it from the table and immediately check for messages, heartache crushing my windpipe when there is nothing. No new call. No new voice mail. No unread text.

Tossing the object on the table I bury my face in my hands. Frustration and gloom grooming my mind. All of sudden my phone starts to vibrate, hope forcing me to hit answer without thinking about it.

Before I can even say hello, a voice I can't wait to never hear again says, "I don't particularly feel like staring at your ear."

After I lower the phone to see his smug smile, I reply through gritted teeth. "I don't particularly like you calling."

"You're gonna love me calling today," his voice tries to entice.

"Doubtful."

"I have a once in a lifetime proposition for you."

"Pass."

"You can." The Devil smirks. "But then your girlfriend dies for sure."

Swallowing the trepidation, I state. "Talk."

"Do you have any idea where I am in this city?" He asks before turning the camera around giving me a view of a landing pad with houses in the far distance.

"I know exactly where you are."

There are two known neighborhoods with landing strips in them. One is the gated neighborhood Azura took me to. The other is almost fifteen minutes from here.

"Good," he says slowly. "Because for someone reason my helicopter has been delayed leaving me stranded here instead of on my way to a different state." The Devil glares. "Could be because someone reported my pilot to the authorities on trumped up charges leaving me with no choice but to call in a last resort to get the hell out of this godforsaken city!"

With a smile I nod. "You're welcome."

"No, no." He wags a finger into the camera. "Not thanking you yet. Burning every known alias I had has ceased me from leaving the country at the moment. That was the play that brought this day to you."

"And what day is that?"

"The day you choose what you want most in life."

My eyebrows furrow.

"I will be here, in this very spot, *alone* and *unarmed* for precisely the next twenty two minutes. You want me dead, McCoy? Come and kill me. With the headache you are beginning to give me, I almost welcome the solitude of death with open arms."

Thrill scoots me to the edge of the couch.

This is it. This is that one moment I've been fucking waiting for. That moment when-

"Or..." he calls to me. "You can save your girlfriend who also has precisely twenty two minutes. The hit man that was hired to take her out is never late."

Vomit lurches up my throat.

"You know where I am. How *far* I am from you. She is the exact same distance in the opposite direction. You can choose one McCoy. Life or death." There's a short cackle before he adds, "Oh and before you rush to have your brothers come to your aid, you should know there's a giant pile up on the freeway. Eighteen wheeler tipped over. No one on that is moving anywhere any time soon."

Divided down the middle with the clock running I meet The Devil's eyes one final time.

"Tick. Tock."

His face disappears and so does my thought process. My phone flies to my pocket, my feet magically end up in a pair of shoes, and the spare gun Madden keeps taped under the kitchen sink is locked and ready for the choice I have to make.

As soon as I'm on my bike with my helmet on, I attempt to call Madden. The phone rings and rings, but no one picks up. I zoom off down the road. I try Knoxie knowing Drew and Melody are cell phone free for the next few hours. Her voicemail kicks on seconds before I pull up to the most horrifying moment of my life. One way I save a life and the other I take it.

Which way would you go? Which fight would you keep swinging for?

Azura

Adjusting my camera lens, I roll my eyes at Jamie's comment. "Why aren't there more women at these things? It's a total sausage fest."

"Because women are usually smart enough to avoid things that can break their necks, not run directly for them," I joke as I lift my device to my eye to capture another behind the scenes shot of Caleb and Cage.

She shrugs. "I don't know. I've met plenty of dumb women in my life."

With another smile I shake my head. Snapping a few more photos in peace is momentary.

"I want a hot dog. Are the shops open yet? Is it too early?"

"Um...I'm not sure." I glance over my shoulder. "Event doesn't start for another couple of hours, so I'm not sure how many vendors are actually open yet. You can feel free to check."

"Want anything if I discover it?"

I shake my head.

227

No appetite with everything rolling around in my head.

Jamie wanders off towards the area of the park set for food while I continue walking around taking snapshots of Caleb and Cage. There are a few other participants here, but primarily it's maintenance people to set up for the event. A smile slides on my face as I watch the entire thing coming together before my eyes, in love with the building adrenaline of the possible history breaking moments that are waiting to be captured.

You know, I really could do this every day. I want to do this every day. I want to make videos and films. I want to edit footage for people like Jamie who are always hesitant to come change their mind about this shit then see it and fall in love. This is what I want to do....why can't I just do it from here?

After lying in bed last night, I decided to turn down the job. Whoa. Whoa. Before you go all Women's Rights on me, I weighed everything and it boiled down to what needs me more. Sure, this may be the only chance I get at some fancy company being paid in more money than I could figure out how to spend, but Destin needs me. He's been through a lot lately. Maybe once he's in a better place we can talk about it again. Kill me if you want for not wanting to give up who I love the most for something I love to do. I can keep doing my job here until we can agree on the timing. It's the least I can do.

He gave me family and a home when I've never had one before. That's more important than any job.

I stop shooting to scroll through the photos I've taken when a maintenance man bumps into me.

"Sorry," I quickly apologize. "I really am trying to stay out of the way."

His dark eyes don't seem to match the rest of the features on his light body. The striking contrast is terrifying. "It's alright." He tries to offer me a warm smile. "What is it you're photographing?"

"Oh just a couple of the skateboarders."

"That's nice. Can I see?"

Cautiously I reply, "Sure."

After I scroll through a few he compliments. "These are really great shots."

"Thanks."

I scroll through a few more, going back when he asks. Eventually the man looks up and states. "I should get back to work. Be careful. Have a nice day."

With a sweet smile I reply, "You as well."

Thankfully he strolls away taking the creepy vibes with him.

Tell me you don't have the chills right now?

A few minutes later I'm headed back towards my bag just as some of the heavy construction noises begin. Curious where Jamie ended up, I reach for my cell phone when a hand abruptly grabs me.

"What the hell?"

Destin who is out of breath for some reason says, "Thank God you're alive."

"Okay you're taking this out of your sight thing a little too far."

"Azura I-" is what comes from him before he yanks me out of the way, a bullet landing in the tree directly beside me. Had he not moved me, my brain would be pinned to that tree. The urge to scream comes flying out, which is when Destin covers my mouth. "Shhh. From that shot my guess is he's closer than you think."

We crouch down together, Destin in front with a gun, me clutching his hand to follow.

Do I even wanna know where the gun came from?

He maneuvers us quickly around using the trees as our shield from the flying shots. Unsure of where the shooting is coming from, I do my best to keep my head down, relieved it's not up to me to get us out of this. Before I know it, we've made it to the other side of the park, closer to the parking lot, right beside the maintenance building.

With our backs up against the wall, Destin lets out a deep sigh. He rolls his head over to me. "Hi..."

"Hi..."

"I'm really glad you're okay."

"Thank you for coming to save me." Feeling like an idiot about the comment I made last night I confess, "I guess I am nothing but a damsel in distress."

He winks. "Not exactly."

I open my mouth to reply when there's a hard object placed against the back of my head.

Horror heaves itself into Destin's eyes as his grip on the gun tightens.

"Drop it," the voice behind me says.

My boyfriend's hand twitches, but doesn't obey. "I don't think so."

"Don't you want the girl to live?" he questions.

"Don't worry," a third voice joins the conversation. I wanna look over my shoulder, but the fear of getting shot because of it keeps me still. "She will."

Suddenly Destin pulls me to him by my hand, the disappearance from the pressure of the gun remarkable. When I'm finally at his side, my eyes fall onto the most unsuspecting face of my rescue.

The creepy maintenance man slowly grabs the gun from the shooter's clutch as he says, "McCoy, I hope you have a license to carry that."

232

"Since I was eighteen, officer," he answers tucking it away.

Really? Creepy man is a cop!

The maintenance man demands of the shooter, "Down on the ground. Nice and slow. Wrong move and I'll let McCoy shoot you in self-defense. No judge would question it."

His tar colored face delivers one more dirty look before he does as the police man says. The officer begins to read him his rights during the process of cuffing him. Once it's done and the man is secured, the cop looks up. "I told you those were great shots." Casually he adds, "His face is all over those photos. Perfect proof."

A smile tries to crawl on my face.

"Get her out of here now. We'll send another unit to watch your place."

"Yes sir," Destin replies, tightening his grip on my hand. "And thank you officer....?"

"Brady," he answers yanking the gunman to his feet. "Just doing my job."

Destin's face turns to me with a smile. "Yeah. Me too..."

Should we write the Police Commissioner a thank you card? Send him a fruit basket? What the hell is the appropriate gift to thank a man for making sure there really is always a cop on me, even when I thought there wasn't? Is it cookies?

Destin

So there's pissed off Madden and then there's Mad Man Madden. Pissed off Madden dents car hood, breaks beer bottles, shatters glass with tools, basically any damage that can be counted in dollars. Mad Man Madden, well he does the kind of damage that haunts a person for a life time. If you're not terrified yet, you should be.

He paces the living room in front of the T.V. "You disobeyed me *again.*"

"Yeah."

"Continued fucking with the *one* person I specifically told you to leave alone, so we wouldn't end up exactly where you did today?"

I sheepishly nod.

"You're fucking mistake could've cost you your life." His hand travels down his face wiping away that wave of anger. "Let me just make sure I understand what happened today. The Devil called and gave you a choice."

"A fucked up one," I comment back. "But yeah. A choice."

235

Madden stops and folds his arms. "And you chose the girl."

My eyes flicker at the girl wound so tightly around me, she's beginning to cut off the circulation in my arm. When I look back at my oldest brother I answer, "I'd choose Azura every time."

It's just like the comic book. Sometimes saving one person saves the whole world...or at least my world.

To my surprise he gives me a smile.

I think he's broken.

"What's wrong with your face?" Knox points out. "It's doing this weird thing. We call it smiling, but yours just...looks infected."

He wipes it away. "Fuck off, Knox."

"That's probably what she was doing this morning, which is why she wasn't here," Drew chuckles at Madden's expense until the death glare moves to him. Quickly he stutters out, "W-w-we know why Mel and I weren't here."

"Where were you?" Knox folds her arms across her chest. "You typically bring your bitch bar trash back to your own bed."

The jealousy in her voice makes the rest of us wince.

Madden states, "I always bring it back home. I won't do the walk of shame for anyone."

"Are you capable of shame?" she snips.

"Can we focus?" Drew interrupts. "If you weren't out fucking last night, why didn't you come home?"

Uncomfortable Madden simply states. "I gave you a check in that I was fine."

Drew quickly argues, "That's not what I asked."

"That's the only information you need."

"That's not fucking right and you know it," Drew growls. "None of us can have secrets. None of us can just fucking disappear when we feel like it. We're all stuck in the house like fucking prisoners because it's what *you* demand! The least you can fucking do is give us some answers!"

Madden tightens his stance. "No."

Silence chokes the life out of the room. Between the tension of unanswered questions and the tension of hurt feelings, it starts to feel like the only way any one will ever breathe again is on life support.

"How did The Devil know you would all be gone?" Azura speaks up. When our attention turns to her she repeats. "How did he know that Destin would be alone?"

A realization that makes me uncomfortable to my core strikes me. "He's watching us." Panicked, I gripe, "He has someone watching the shop."

"No," Drew denies quickly. "You swept for bugs. You keep sweeping for bugs. You're security feed would've picked up something."

"Traffic cameras," Mel whispers. "The one closest to the shop. The one we have to pass through when coming or going. He could tap into that to watch for your vehicles."

"But why offer Destin the chance to kill him?" Azura questions.

"It wasn't a real offer," Madden growls. "He was fucking with him. He was proving the point that no matter what we do, he's always going to be ahead of us. No matter what happens, we won't risk hurting someone we love to hurt something we hate."

"He may not always be ahead," I mumble grabbing everyone's eyes.

Displeased by the remark Madden demands, "Explain."

"A few days ago when the BV MC member came by, she mentioned something that I....was waiting to tell you." Drew shakes his head at me. Timidly I apologize, "Sorry, Big D. I just...I didn't wanna take the risk until I knew more."

"You lied to my face."

"You knew I lied to your face."

"Is that why you were so upset that day?" Mel asks him.

"What's the information I'm waiting to beat the shit out of you over," Madden says sharply.

That ass whooping is gonna hurt.

"If Azura swears she doesn't remember anything-"

"I really don't!" she squeaks.

"And we can return something they're missing as a peace offering, they'll leave her alone."

"Something they're missing?" Knox questions. "They're a gang. How does something just go missing? And do you look like the Hardy boys? Where does it say you like to pull out your magnifying glasses and solve mysteries?"

Don't encourage her by laughing.

"A token they stole from another gang went missing a few years ago. I figured if I could find out what it was, we could make a forgery, give it to them, and everybody would win. I just...I had to figure out what it was first."

Madden questions sternly, "And did you?"

"Yeah." I reach for my phone and scroll through the pictures until I find it. "It's this."

Holding the screen up Drew grunts, "Is that a shirt barrette?"

"Brooch," Knox corrects him. "And no. It's not."

"It's a diamond scorpion cuff link," I inform everyone. "It wouldn't be that hard to recreate."

A look I don't recognize comes across Madden's face. "There's no need to."

"No need to what?" Knox asks.

"Fake it. I know exactly where it is."

Blown away how that's even a possibility, I snap, "What?"

"What do you mean you know where it is?" Drew echoes.

"How do you know?" Knox joins the conversation.

Madden hums to himself. "I'll explain later. For now...I have a plan."

You know, usually when there are this many McCoys all in the same room at the same time and there's not dinner or a party involved, it means the worst has happened or is about to. For everyone's sake, I hope for once, it's just the opposite.

Destin

Sitting wedged between my two brothers at the long wooden table, I hold my composure knowing the smallest sign of weakness sensed by them will turn things ugly.

Turns out BV MC is even scarier in person. Just in case you're wondering.

Slaughter taps his thumbs together. "I'm here. Neutral territory. That's smart McCoy."

"Being dumb gets you killed," Madden informs coldly.

"You know," he starts, still tapping his thumbs together. "I bet you'd make a helluva MC member."

"Bet I wouldn't," my big brother counters. "Now, to business. You're an important man. You don't have time to waste."

"I don't." He agrees. "So talk."

His entire presence is as fucking intimidating as Madden's except instead of being brunette he's blond. Like my brother who has a jagged scar along his jawbone, Slaughter has one that runs across his neck. It looks like someone tried to slice him open and failed. I don't wanna know what happens to failures who try to kill men like them.

"I wanna cut a deal," Madden announces.

Slaughter's fingers tap together again. "I like deals. Particularly when they have a price tag. Does yours?"

"A big one," Madden assures. "Destin."

Putting my tablet on the table, I tab over to the first set of documents.

"That is a sworn testimony from the woman you are hunting down stating she has no memory, no recollection of the crime you allegedly committed. She does not recall you leaving the scene. She does not remember your name, your face, or even being there at that time." When my finger swipes over Madden continues, "This is the law in which would be used by your lawyer to prevent a two decade old memory from holding merit in court."

The large man on his left, his VP to my understanding, leans over his shoulder. "Do you want me to call our guy to verify that?"

Slaughter holds a finger to him to shut the man up. "Continue."

When Madden tosses me a nod, I tab over a few to another document that looks damn near identical to the first. "*This* is a sworn testimony from the woman you are hunting down that says she recalls the crime in perfect detail. She describes the entire afternoon vividly, including you leaving the house of ZD President on the day of his murder." After I tab over he adds, "And this is the law in which the prosecution will use that very testimony that can no longer get you charged for the original alleged crime of theft, but can be used against you for the open homicide investigation."

"There's no statute of limitations on murder," Drew inserts. "But you knew that."

The growl from the man across the table is followed by the sucking of his teeth. "That's not exactly honorable McCoy."

"Protecting family first," he states. "And I think that's the honor that matters most to you doesn't it?"

Slaughter doesn't disagree.

"We'll give you a copy of her testimony that says she has no recollection *and* something you want that's been missing for quite some time."

His eyes light up. He rocks in his seat. "And what do you want in exchange, McCoy?"

"The girl left alone. For good." Madden starts. "And a favor."

Slaughter leans back. "I'm not big on favors."

Slowly Madden leans forward. "This one comes with a price tag."

"And I like those." Slaughter sly smirks. "Alright McCoy. You have my complete attention now. What's the favor?"

Oh it's a good one....You'll see.

Azura

Flustered I snip, "Damn it, Destin! Hand me the tape!"

"What tape?" He wiggles his empty fingers at me. "I don't see any tape."

On a defeated sigh I whine, "You are turning a two day packing job into a two week one."

"Drama queen," he grunts and tosses me the dispenser that he had tucked in his pants. "You're lucky I love you."

"That I am." When he smiles at me, I lean over and give him a quick kiss. "But that doesn't mean you get to torture me while you're supposed to be helping me pack."

"It's hard enough I have to see you go." Destin flops down on the edge of my bare mattress. "I really don't like the idea of being the one to help you do it."

Leaning against my dresser I reply, "I know."

After the park incident, Madden came up with a plan that freed me from the fear of the BV MC. Once it was all settled, Destin broke down and begged me to take the job. I told them I would take

246

it on the condition that I could work from home unless it was a requirement to travel. Marshal agreed but demanded I still spend the first couple of months in London for training. Destin agreed he could live with a traveling girlfriend as long as I came back to him and without the fear of the BV MV waiting around every corner to kill me, I think I'm okay with it too. Doesn't make actually having to leave the person who is going to miss me most any easier. Even if it is temporary.

"You're pretty cute when you're pouting," I whisper.

Destin smiles and beckons me to come closer. He pulls me into his lap. With my arms wrapped around him, I smile at his head on my shoulder.

"I promise everything will be okay."

"I'm gonna miss you," he says quietly. "I feel like I just got you and now I'm losing you."

"But you're not." I lift his chin. "You're just sharing me with a bunch of adrenaline junkie sports fiends."

"You know when I thought about group sex that's not quite how I pictured it." His chuckling gets mine going as well as a playful elbow. "You're gonna be amazing at this."

247

"I sure hope so."

With a crooked smile he says, "I have faith in you."

A swoon comes from me before I push our mouths together, lips locking tightly. Instead of feeling frenzied when his tongue knocks against my bottom lip, there's a different kind of hunger. This one is begging me to absorb every inch of him I can before I leave in two days. The kiss is shorter than I care, but admittedly for the best.

My parents are back and making us a goodbye/good luck/nice to meet you dinner. It was Destin's idea in an attempt to show them how much he cares about me even though they don't seem to. Wouldn't be the wisest to sneak a quickie in with them just down the hall. Especially not with as loud as we get.

"You ready for your going away present?"

"I can't in good conscious unwrap that with my parents in the next room."

Destin lets out a dirty snicker before shaking his head. "No. Not that. I mean you can unwrap that any time and all the time, but I got you an actual gift."

"Really?" My smirk grows. "Because I got you one too."

"Huh," he says in disbelief. "Really?"

"Yeah." I stand to retrieve it from the top shelf in my closet. "But you can't, I repeat, cannot open it until I am on the plane."

"Or..."

Reaching for it I reply, "Or there will be no Skype sex for the first two weeks."

"Aw man," he grumbles. "Fine."

When I turn around with the small square box wrapped in red paper, I see him holding a long one covered in newspaper. Placing his down on the edge of my bed, I take mine into my hands.

"I don't know if you can take it with you, but um...if you can't, I'll just...I'll just hold onto it until you get back."

Slowly I tear off the paper and toss away the lid. Inside the long box is a brand new black skateboard. The custom design on the bottom is red as well as one I know very well. Seeing it drops me onto my bed while tears strangle my throat.

Destin slips his hands into his pocket. "When you first asked me to design something for your board, I wanted something cool and innovative. But then time went on and I fell in love with you. Suddenly I wanted something original. Meaningful." He clears his throat. "I have that mark. Drew has that mark. Daniel had that mark."

A tear falls onto the treasure in my lap.

"You're the reason I'm still alive. You made yourself known in my life at exactly the right moment in time. I was...just a couple bottles away from no longer existing and you breathed life back into me. You helped clean up my world. You...you fucking gave me a world I wanted to not only live in but fight in for another day with you. So...Azura Rose, you are the heartbeat of this McCoy."

Unsure of what to say, I toss the board down and rush over to him. The kiss this time is frantic, on fire, but it's the kind of scorching heat that fuses two people together. His arms cradle me just as his mouth does. Hard. Intense. Lovingly.

Do you see now why I'd give up my dream job for my dream love? While I'm thankful I don't have to, never forget, if I had to choose all over again, I'd still choose him.

Destin

Entering the apartment I smile at the sight of my family gathered around the T.V. This moment like the one before that final boss fight in every video game.

Except this one is going to be so much better.

"Get her put on the plane?" Madden asks from Knox's side.

"I did," I confirm pushing my sorrow down.

Now's not the time. Now's the time for smiles. For fucking pats on the back.

"It's okay to be a little mushy about letting her go," Knox encourages.

"You did the right thing," Drew sighs as I sit beside him.

"I know."

He tosses his arm around my shoulder. "She'll be back before you know it."

"Unless she meets some British billionaire who whisks her away to live in his flat full time," Knox's joke gets all of our harshest glares. "Oh...come on! It was a joke. Remove tampons *then* laugh."

It wasn't funny though. Wait, do you think that'll actually happen? Should I call and leave her a voicemail right now? Should I send her a text? Maybe a picture?

"Look what you did," Drew fusses at her. "You sent Triple D into panic mode." He gives me a good squeeze. "Stop plotting ways to hack into her computer to leave her creepy but loving sentiments."

Rolling my eyes I shrug him off of me.

Madden reaches for the remote, a very strong sense of pride plastered on his face. "Where's Mel?"

"Napping," he informs. "Told her to text me before she tries to come out if I haven't already joined her."

"How can you possibly be that tired already?" Knox grills. "You worked like half a shift at the shop yesterday."

"And then another half between my woman's legs." Drew holds a hand up. "Look, it's exhausting work, but someone has to do it."

252

"Could you McCoys like *not* do it for a small fraction of time? There are so many sexual sounds in this apartment, wild animals have started to travel for miles towards the noise. I swear, the next thing I know you're all gonna be on The Discovery Channel."

In my best T.V. show voice I say, "The tall dark and handsome McCoy is highly wanted in the wilderness."

Knox gags. "Oh I wish you were, so I could be a hunter, shoot you both, and wear you as bikinis."

The two of us laugh together which is when Madden interjects, "I don't want either of their body parts on...any of your body parts."

He's gotta come clean eventually right? How long can he get away saying shit like that without actually manning up to the plate?

"That's what you have a problem with?" Knox snaps. "Not the hunting or skinning of the Triple D-"

"That's bound to happen," Drew jokes and I laugh with him before we bump fists.

"Shut up," Madden demands at us. When he looks back at Knox he says, "We're about to get started. You sure you wanna be a part of this?"

Knoxie stares at my big brother the way she does when she has to stop herself from either killing him or professing her love.

Is it weird that it's the same fucking face?

"I'm *already* a part of this," she counters. "Do it."

Madden twitches a small smirk before he turns to me. "Triple D."

"Yup." I reach for my computer on the coffee table while he turns to the channel. After the typing of a few keys the back of The Devil's chair appears.

"Surprise." Madden states coldly.

No. He couldn't even be enthusiastic about it.

Slowly the chair turns around revealing The Devil's expressionless face. "McCoys. Well you're all still alive so this conversation is not going to be as much fun as I was hoping."

Drew and I fight the urge to tense at that comment.

He clasps his hands together staring at us from his computer screen. "What do you want?" His eyes wander over to me. "I mean...you had the chance to kill me and *lost* it." The pretend shock face he makes pushes my buttons. "So what could this possibly be about?"

Madden answers, "You."

With a twirl of his hand he agrees, "I am a fantastic subject."

"Your days are numbered."

"They always are," he retorts. "Is that why you called Madden? To remind me you're still miles behind, chasing me like the Pitbull after the Viper. Because I have to be frank with you. I'm growing bored."

"No," Madden states. "You're not. You're growing scared." When The Devil lifts his eyebrows he says, "The BV MC is no longer an issue."

Hopeful, he questions, "Killed the girl?"

I prepare to lunge forward when Drew taps my foot reminding me to stay cool. "Better."

"What do you mean better?"

"They protect her now." My information causes him to frown. "In fact, they protect all of us."

The Devil leans back in his chair. "What's that now?"

"You heard him," Drew echoes. "All of us."

"See while you're so focused on the big fish you have floating around, you've forgotten the little ones," Madden explains. "The small pushers. The small dealers. The small suppliers. You were so fucking desperate to save the big one's The Commissioner knew about you neglecting   them and now that your business is in a choke hold you're gonna want them more than ever. Problem is...they don't belong to you anymore."

"They're the BV MC's now," Knoxie proudly smirks.

He tries to hold it together but there's frustration steadily building. The sight makes me want to smile again.

"I have list after list from *years* of working under you. Names. Places. Routes. Times. Rotations. I sold them all to the BV MC for a low price. They agreed to move major distribution out of the city and do their best to insure that this at least looks clean enough for tax payers to sleep at night. I owe the Commissioner a favor or two. It'll make him look good."

"Is that it?"

"Well of course not. I mean a market this big to clean up, I knew I could get more. Oh and in case you're curious, everyone you worked with, switched with damn near no hesitation. Same cuts. Same deals. Except they know if something goes south, BV MC protects their own. Down to the petty pusher. They're honorable men."

"Unlike you," Knox adds.

"They agreed to keep us watched over while we hunt you down. They're not particularly fond of you. Not only for how poorly you treat the men who should defend instead of destroy, but for taking something that never belonged to you."

Suddenly The Devil's eyes light up. "Oh yeah? What's that?"

Madden smiles. "A simple cuff link."

When he receives the information he grouses, "That was worth millions."

"It's worth *so* much more than that," Madden corrects. "Saved a McCoy's life. That makes the thing fucking priceless. I'll never forget the day you gave that shit to me and told me to keep it safe because some day I would need it." With a head tilt he says, "You were right."

"You were using Madden to hide it," Drew states. "Because you knew if the BV MC ever found out you had it, they wouldn't hesitate to kill you."

"Stealing from an MC?" Knoxie fusses. "Tsk. Tsk."

"Do you know how they got that cuff link?" I join in. "It was chopped off the president of the ZD MC's hand. Took the cuff as a trophy. The action was meant to instill fear. Act as a reminder that they were the best. Having it stolen from underneath their noses brought them a level of shame and dishonor."

"Did we mention how they feel about honor?" Drew chortles.

"They already didn't like you for the *dishonorable* way you've treated us, but when we added to the mix the very thing they were lacking was stolen by *you*, well...it didn't take much convincing to have them on our side." Madden leans in closer. "They wanted your blood for themselves, but being that they are respectable men, they bestowed that right upon me for the lives you've take from us."

For the first time I recall The Devil looks speechless.

"In about forty five seconds, the cops are gonna tear through your front door. They're going to arrest your body guard. Question your driver. Scare the shit out of your maids. They're going to shred that house limb from limb looking for you," Drew warns.

"And you're on your last resources asshole," I add. "Every dealer willing to listen has been passed the information to *not* make you a new passport to leave the country. Some won't on favors to us, most won't because of the death threat that comes with it from BV."

"No money. No cars. No planes. No houses." Knoxie states sharply. "Life is about to get a little rough."

Madden leans forward towards the T.V. "I'm coming for you motherfucker."

The Devil shuts his computer off leaving us with a black screen. With a wide smile I look over at Drew who fists bumps me.

Out of the corner of my eye, I see Knox give Madden the lightest of strokes on his back. His head drops for a brief second.

That has to be the most amount of relief I've seen on his face in weeks.

"When we finally bring him down it's gonna be epic," Drew sighs.

"No." Madden lifts his back up. "I'm gonna make that shit fucking iconic."

We all nod in agreement an eerie calmness arriving. After a few moments of silence pass, I grab the wrapped box I was told to wait to open.

Hey. I waited long enough! If I wait any longer Drew might open it for me. He's done it before. He's a pain in the ass at Christmas.

Drew tilts his head at it. "Going away gift?"

"Yeah."

"Maybe it's a blow up doll that looks like her," Knoxie jokes.

"Maybe it's these magical things you stick in your ears, so you can only hear what she's saying!" Drew exclaims.

"Those are called headphones."

"Yeah. Use 'em. I don't wanna hear Skype sex every night."

"Our rooms aren't even that close."

"You're loud!"

"You're loud!" I snap back.

"You're all loud. We discussed this already. I'm putting a call into The Animal Planet about it," Knoxie sighs. "Now open the damn thing."

"It's been taunting me from the coffee table for two days. Open it," Drew backs her.

Quickly I shred the paper and open the box surprised at the small flash drive inside.

Drew leans over. "Very anticlimactic."

"That's what she said," Knox giggles and Drew laughs with a nod.

"It's something she'll never have to say 'cause she's fucking a McCoy," I correct Knox.

I cross over to plug the drive into the T.V.

"What if it's video porn?" Drew ponders. "Do you really want us all here to watch?"

Grabbing the remote on the way back to the couch I snap, "It's not porn moron."

"Yeah. When chicks do it, it's called an X-rated video," Knoxie sighs.

Drew starts laughing and Madden fusses. "Why do you encourage him?"

"To watch your forehead wrinkle."

The declaration does, which makes us laugh again.

"Look whatever it is, Azura said make sure you guys were around for it."

"Well get the thing going," Drew huffs. "I'm getting antsy."

"You mean horny?" Madden questions extending his arm around the back of the couch behind Knox.

"Same. Same."

Through a chuckle I manage to get the video pulled up.

Azura's beautiful face appears on the screen. She's positioned on the edge of my bed. The sight of her in a jean skirt and sweater makes my heart heavy.

Fuck. This is going to be the longest two months of my life.

"Hi McCoys," she coos into the screen.

Instinctively I say back, "Hi..."

"She can't hear you," Knox states.

"Let me have it," Drew encourages.

"So....I know having me come into your lives was probably a bigger deal than you imagined it would be." She starts nervously, which makes me smile. "But I truly appreciate everything you did for me. Have done for me. Will probably continue to do. You are the most amazing people in the entire world and I can never thank you enough, not only for saving my life, but for letting me become a member of your family, especially since I didn't really have one."

There's a small pause as she smiles brightly into the camera.

I swear it's just for me.

"I left for the airport today, unless Destin was a bad boy in which I haven't left yet and he's gonna be in huge trouble." Chuckling I fold my arms across my chest. "I know you've lost a lot in these past few months. I know it's been hard. More importantly I know you fear the idea of forgetting. Of letting those memories just...die. But as someone who has an entire life they'll never be able to know about or get back, I will say no one deserves to feel that. You deserve to keep those memories forever. So here you go...my thank you to you. And my I love you to you Destin..."

Drew looks at me. "Is she gonna sing?"

Knox groans, "God I hope she doesn't sing."

"If she fucking sings, I'm turning it off," Madden declares.

There's a brief second of a black screen before a face appears that sends us all to the edge of our seat.

"I'm a fucking McCoy," Daniel chuckles goofy into the camera. "What's better than that baby!" The girl beside him tosses her hands in the air seconds before doing a shot with him.

"That's fucking Middle Man," Drew whispers weakly.

The video footage cuts to another shot of Daniel being the life of a different party. We watch as the world cheers him, Merrick laughing at his side. More drinks are had, more laughs captured, the two of them looking like drunken idiots, but happy nonetheless. The film changes scenes again this time to the three of us at a pool party. We're laughing hysterically, trying to drown each other, chicks desperately trying to be close to us.

A female voice I don't recognize says, "Another day in the life of a McCoy."

It zooms in on the three of us together, leaned against the edge, smiles never fading. Suddenly it fades to footage of us working in the shop together. Merrick is play fighting with Ben. I'm in the office on the phone. Drew's talking to Madden and Knox. There's no audio, but by the smiles we're giving off it was probably a good day. Daniel slides out from underneath a Benz he was working on, laughing while Knox smirks and Madden scowls.

Some things never change.

The montage changes to Daniel doing a performance on his bike at one of the events he used to attend. It shows him completing several stunts, the crowd eating him up, demanding more from him. After his final trick he parks and simply waits for something. That's when it happens, he's joined by two more motorcycles. One on each side.

"That's us," Drew whispers with tears on his face.

In unison the three of us take off down the road and pop up onto one wheel at the exact same time. The video stills at that moment capturing the three of us the way I'll never forget. As one unit.

With tears on my own face at the sight of the three us together, forever frozen in time, I lean back with a bittersweet smile on my face as I read the words out loud. "Thank you for welcoming me into the best family in the world."

Dead or alive. That fact is true. Even if Daniel, Ben, and Merrick are not here beside us, they're still family. They're still a part of us. And thanks to the most amazing woman I've met in my life, I can see us together any time. How she even found all this footage is beyond me. I don't even fucking care. All that matters is now we have it. We have a solid piece of history no one can take from us. Damn it feels to be a McCoy. Like Middle Man said...what's better than that?

Epilogue

Azura

Gripping my bag tighter, I slide into the front seat of the SUV Destin is driving. Thankful to be out of the cold I buckle up and rub my hands together while he loads my bags.

As soon as he's all done he slips back in the driver's seat. "Fuck...my nuts are so frozen I feel like I should be roasting them on an open fire."

The joke makes me snicker before leaning over to give him another kiss.

We may have made out right outside the door for a few minutes before he grabbed my bags. Can you blame us? I haven't seen him in two months and there is only so much a vibrator can do. Though if you must know Destin has declared that as an 'only while working away from him' object. He preached and preached about how he will make sure my pussy is too worn out to ever need it when I'm home. Is it wrong to hope he makes good on his promise?

Destin pulls away and leans his forehead against mine. "Hi..."

With a bright smile, I coo back, "Hi..."

Another peck makes it onto my mouth before he pulls out of park and away from the airport. "Glad to be home?"

I reach over and drop my hand on his lap. "Glad to be back with you."

There's a long groan that comes from him. "Careful. I am not above pulling this car over into an empty parking lot, letting the seats down, and having a quickie before dinner at The Commissioner's house."

Weird I know, but when he requested this one thing from us we couldn't really deny him. I mean all he did to save me from the BV MC before they came to peaceful terms with the McCoys? That cop who saved my life when there was a gun to my head? All the pulls he made to keep me safe, I couldn't just tell him no, when we were requested for dinner. It's the least we can do no matter how much I wish we were home at the apartment having wild and crazy glad to be home sex.

Changing subjects I ask, "Aside from being ridiculously horny, how is everything? How's the tattoo designing coming along?"

"It's really fucking awesome..."

About a week after I left, during one of our nightly video calls, Destin showed me some of his doodles. While most of the designs were the typical cartoon characters or me topless, he had a few that he liked for tattoo possibilities if he were to ever go back and get another one. He explained how he wanted one that could stand for the all McCoys they've lost. None had really made the cut yet, but it got my mind working. A couple days later, I gave him the number of a tattoo shop I knew through Cage that was looking for a new artist. Next thing I knew Destin's doodles were turned from absentminded drawings into a profitable hobby. It's not like he needs the cash, but he enjoys the escape it creates. There's still some rough moments when Daniel's death hurts too bad or Merrick's lack of presence springs into mind. Those are the time he's needs me most. Each time it happened and he broke down I had to talk myself off the ledge of coming home to hold him. However, we eventually began to agree it was good he had some space to learn to cope. To stand on his own two feet again. I think part of him needed that independence. Besides, with The Devil finally dead, I think it's easier for him to gain it.

"I think I might've settled on one for all of us."

Confused I question. "All of us? By all of us you mean-"

270

"You. Me. Madden. Knox. Drew. And Mel. All the McCoys."

My mouth moves, but nothing comes out.

"You don't want a tattoo?"

"Not really," I squeak. "Needles kind of freak me out."

"Needles?"

"Yes."

"Watching free runs and boogie boarding with sharks is all very normal to you but *needles* freak you out?"

I give his leg a squeeze. "Keep up that kind of lip and you won't be giving me any other kind."

Destin groans and pounds the steering wheel in sexual frustration.

After a giggle I sigh, "Okay, but seriously. You want us all to get the same one?"

"Yeah." He glances over at me. "It would mean a lot to me." The look in his eyes has me nibbling on my bottom lip. "But...if you're too scared, I understand. I'll have Drew figure out how to make you one of those cheap out of the machine washable ones." Before I can snap again he says, "Speaking of Drew, how do you like his SUV?"

"I'm glad it's his."

He frowns. "You don't like it?"

"I don't like *you* in it."

"What? Why not?"

"I don't know. I guess I prefer my Destin on two wheels..." I seductively say.

Another growl comes from him. "You're killing me baby..."

With a short snicker I check the time, trying to estimate how long until sex o'clock.

Look. I have needs too...

"Don't worry about that. Me and Pepper are still together. This was just to keep you warm and get all your shit back to the apartment in the least amount of trips. Now do me a favor and open the glove compartment."

I follow his request seeing a small velvet box with a red bow. An unhappy look pops up on my face. "We said we were waiting to exchange presents until after dinner."

"We are," he says. "This is just an early one. Open it."

"But Destin-"

"Open it."

Rolling my eyes, I grab the box, pull at the ribbon and open it. Inside there's a shiny silver key. When I look up, I'm thankful we are at a stoplight. I lift it up and twirl it around my fingers. "Sex dungeon?"

He chuckles. "If that's what you wanna call our new apartment, you have my full support."

Shock invades my system. "Our what?"

"Apartment." My jaw bobs to object. "I realized when you came home I wanted you to come home to *our* home. I also figured, it's gonna be a lot harder to get past my brothers and cousin's deaths if every time I'm in the apartment it feels like I'm looking at their gravestones. This will be good for me. For you. For us."

I press my lips together for a moment as I slip the key back into the box. "Are you sure that's what you want? A new home?"

"As long as I'm with you baby, anywhere is home."

I know the feeling. I guess that's the craziest thing about love. Once you find it, I mean really find it, you never feel homeless or lost again. I may have grown up feeling awkward, with barely there parents and a distant sibling, but I know now, what's truly important. What having family really feels like. I now know exactly what it feels like to have a home.

THANK YOUS

Crazy Lady- Your after you've finished reading phone calls are some of my favorites!

Her Husband- Not too shabby for the baby huh?

The Law Student- Weakly phone calls. Get on it. Lol

The Lumberjack- For feeding me Tex Mex when I need it, I love you.

Nanny Job- For letting me have a stable job while writing takes off.

Sissy B- Hope these books make you smile.

Katniss- So....who do you love the most now? lmao

The Real Life Erin- Keep up that Pretty Girl Rock.

Throwback- I love our dates...gotta keep 'em up!

The PAs- Left and Right brain, I appreciate that even when times get tight and rough you're both still there for me.

The Editor- Squishy hugs for never killing me over deadlines.

Boss Lady- Double for what I said to The Editor, lol. I love you for understanding I need sleep.

Genie- You should star in Aladdin 4! I love that only you and I get this joke.

To the writer's I admire- The list changes and grows every day, but here is my special thank you to all of you. You are wonderful.

Dream Team- Thanks for always understanding what 'in the cave' really means.

Patrice H- For loving my books and giving them your time, your reviews, and your energy. I thank you for appreciating my approach to IR instead of ripping it apart for not being "enough" of something.

Cka R- Your wedding gift is in the mail, haha. Thank you for being part of my writing family and one of the only times from my early days that didn't turn into something sucky.

Bloggers- Every time you answer a message or a request for me or for others you give this industry hope for indies. Thank you!

Readers- Last, but never least. There's no real way I can thank you enough for the endless support, but I promise to never stop trying. Thanks for the reviews too! I really do read them all.

Until next time....

Curious about what happened to the Merrick McCoy?

Make sure you check out his books:

Classic
Vintage
Masterpiece

Want to hear about how Drew and Mel fell in love?

Make sure to check out his standalone novel:

Unmask

Curious how The Devil is finally taken down? Ready to see Knox and Madden explode on the page?

Look out for 'Iconic' COMING SOON!

Books by Xavier Neal

Senses Series:
Vital (Prequel) Found in Interwoven
Blind (Book 1)
Deaf (Book 2
Numb (Book 3)
Hush (Book 4)
Savor (Book 5)
Callous (Book 6)
Agonize (Book 7)
Suffocate (Book 8)
Mollify (Book 9)
Senses Series Box Set (Books 1-5)

Havoc Series
Havoc (Book 1)
Chaos (Book 2)
Insantity (Book 3)
Collapse (Book 4)
Devastate (Book 5)
Havoc Series Box Set (Books 1-3)

Never Say Neverland
Get Lost
Lost in Lies
Lies Mistrust and Fairy Dust

Adrenaline Series
Classic
Vintage
Masterpiece
Unmask
Error

Connect with Xavier Neal

Amazon:http://www.amazon.com/XavierNeal/e/B00IY1FRY

Links: www.xavierneal.com

Facebook:
https://www.facebook.com/XavierNealAuthorPage

Twitter: @XavierNeal87

Goodreads:https://www.goodreads.com/author/show/499013
5.Xavier_Neal

Interested in joining my newsletter so you don't miss a thing?
Send me a quick email with your email address to be added!

Follow Entetwine Publishing for more great books
Facebook: www.facebook.com/Entertwinepub
Twitter: @Entertwine1
Goodreads:https://www.goodreads.com/user/show/34469714-entertwine-publishing
Or join our mailing list. Sign up is easy and we never share or sell your information. You will receive monthly newsletters debuting new covers, upcoming releases, author interviews and more. Sign up here: http://goo.gl/forms/bwQuKcxSFr

Made in the USA
Columbia, SC
04 July 2018